Naked Truth

Jordan Sarah Weatherhead

Photographs by Shawn Rode

Present in the photographs is author
Jordan Sarah Weatherhead

ISBN: 1449980376
ISBN-13: 9781449980375

"I'm not afraid of the things you know
I'm just a book for the world to read
My final words on the final page
Will be your name 'cause I believe"
Blind as a Bat by Meatloaf

More than a million thank you's and endless love to Chad
and Courtney. One inspired this book and one encouraged
and nourished it. I thank Chad for also supplying me
with the chapter quotes along our journey; you don't
even know it but everything you say, stays.

xxx

A huge thank you to Shawn Rode for all of your illustrations
and the cover art you created for this book. You are
a rare and beautiful person. I so am blessed to have
such a talented and honest person in my life.

xxx

Also a HUGE thank you to Great Grandpa Weatherhead for
leaving your poetry behind for me to discover and use in my
book. I never got to know you but I feel like we are a lot alike.
I learned so much through your timeless words. Send my
love to all the others up there that I've lost along the way.

xxx

"Hope is never really lost, just misplaced." –JSW

Warning:
May contain graphic material.

Table of Contents

Distance & Deployment

"We gotta go through hell to get to Heaven" ~CCV

5 Senses

I felt your hand today
When I was driving home
I looked to the passenger side
But I was alone

I heard your voice today
When I was on the phone
But when I listened for more
Dial tone

I smelled your scent today
When I walked through the door
Then I walked a little further
And smelt it no more

I tasted your lips today
When I bit into a sugarplum
Then I bit in again
But my tongue went numb

I saw you today
You were right in front of me
.....
Then I realized
it was all a dream
.....
And all at once
my heart stopped beating

After I Die...

The mere mention of your name and I go insane
I think this must be the best kind of pain
Red eyes, shaky hands, aching of my back and head
I think maybe I should just take some Tylenol and go to bed...

The phone rings and I jump out of my skin
How long has it been?
I've been sitting here for years, or so
it seems, waiting for your call
When I jumped, I didn't realize how hard I'd fall
I guess I didn't even know you at all...

Turning into an insomniac
Waiting to have you back
Seconds pass and days go by
I'll wait for you, even after I die...

American Soldiers

This is for the red white and blue
Has any of this affected you?
If you say no then you're wrong
It's been affecting you all along
Every thing these heroes do and say
Affects your freedom in every way
For hundreds of years they've fought and they've died
For hundreds of years, millions have cried
Every soldier has protected and tried
Some have fallen, some survived
Is it your sister, your father, your friend, your brother?
Are you in fear of losing your daughter,
son, your boyfriend, or your mother?
Do you wear the uniform proudly or are you just their family?
Either way, we thank you immensely
Does the USA flag mean anything to you?
Do you even think about the colors Red White and Blue?
Is today the only day you thank them?
Is Veterans Day the only day you think
about our brave women and men?
I think we should all rethink this day...

And realize we should be this grateful EVERYDAY
I'm so proud of my husband and his friends
And all the uniformed women and men
And all the families and daughters and sons
Who are waiting for mommy and daddy
to put down their guns
Hearing my son ask for his daddy day and night
Doesn't feel fair and it doesn't seem right
But when I get to tell him what an important job he's doing
It suddenly feels right and it's just so moving
I feel pride everyday for my husband overseas
And I just ask of all of you please:
Thank the soldiers who make you free
Because those two little words mean everything
My husband's been gone for over 200 days
It's a lifestyle we all lead, not just a phase
So take some time just to sit and think...
That with out our American Soldiers,
this country would sink...

Approaching

My heart is starting to beat a little faster
The last few months have become a blur
The end is nearing and my body is warm
I just hope we'll last, hope I haven't caused too much harm

The story of our lives, is you leaving
Then I lie on the floor, pain in chest, and dry heaving
Distance makes my heart grow fonder
So, I'll never get sick of you
You're gone far too much for me to know what to do

There is a rock in my throat because it's the 1st now
I need to slow down the days somehow
Quick sand them or slow them down with a rope
Searching, but hard to find is my hope

I have no confidence that I won't cry
To say that I would try not to is a terrible lie
I'll let the tears fall until no more will come
Then maybe, just maybe, my pain will succumb

Can You?

Can you see my fire burning?
From 1,000 miles away?
I feel desire and I yearn
Day after sorrowful day
Look out your window, what do you see?
Do you notice my fire and me?
It burns bright throughout the night
Are these words becoming trite?

Can you feel my breath?
From 1,000 miles away?
The thought of you feels like death
Only because it takes my breath away
Don't move, just stand still
Can you feel my breath?
Can you feel the chill?
I breathe so heavy when I think of you
Open your mouth and breathe too

Can you hear me whisper?
From 1,000 miles away?
Even though I'm not in sight
Can you hear what I say?
Be quiet, don't make a sound
Tell me, do you hear my words?
Do they shake your ground?
I talk to you when I am awake and when I am asleep
Now I know what I have to do...I think...

Cold, Heat, & Color

I wandered out into the bitter cold
I wandered out into the snow
The bite of the chill scratched at my face
With out you, I felt unsafe

I took off my jacket, then my gloves and my hat
And screamed into the night, that I just want you back
I'd rather feel the pain of this cold then
live with the pain of not having you
So I try to cover up my emotions with something new...

I wandered out into the dessert storm
It was a fucking melting pot, not just warm
The heat lashed out at my skin
As I let the torture seep in

I put on my jacket, then my gloves and my hat
And screamed into the sun, that I just want you back
I'd rather feel the pain of this scorching heat
than live with the pain of not having you
So I try to cover up my emotions with something new...

I wandered into the bar and ordered a drink
Then I turned off my brain so I wouldn't have to think
I let the liquor burn my throat all the way down
In hopes that maybe some of this aching would drown

I ordered every drink, and made them top shelf
And screamed into the glass that if I can't
have you, I don't want anybody else
I'd rather feel the pain of this awful hangover
than live with the pain of not having you
So I tried to cover up my emotions with something new...

I try not to let myself cry anymore
I replace it with cold and heat and glasses full of color
I'd rather replace this all with something different,
something pointless, something new
Than live in agony for a second when I remember
how long it's been since I've had you...

For Just One Day

Move me from this place
Lift me up and take me away
Drop me off somewhere new
Then drop him off too

Paint the background crimson and gold
Maybe add some blues
Make the music soft and airy
Give us some dancing shoes

Make his suit a sharp charcoal
Dress me up in a gorgeous gown
I only want the ring he gave me
But place on his head, a crown

Put the skies on fire as the sun sets
And have sweet flowers all around
Have butterscotch smells in the air
And put some vibrant sand on the ground

The temperature, make it eighty
But make sure that there's a breeze
And let us be alone
I ask this of you, please

Have him kiss me and tell me I'm the only one
Have the words ring soft and true
Let his hand brush across my skin
Have him whisper gently, I love you

Move me from this place
Somewhere with my best friend
My soul mate
Lift me up and take me away
Even if it is for just one day. . .

Funny Pain

Tears run down my face as I smile
I've been wanting this for a while
Laughter fills my lungs as I cry
My legs are numb and I know exactly why

Sitting here dreaming of that in this solitude
I try to get up to walk, but I'm in no mood
Laying in these days of purgatory
You don't even know half the story

My pain cuts through me like a million shards of glass
And I chuckle like a clown in laughing gas
Hysteria sets in and I start to go insane
Psychotic poison flowing through my veins

I sit here unsociably active
Crying because I'm so unattractive
Criticizing my every curve and defect
Feeling useless, disgusting, and completely ship-wrecked

Suffocating on the emptiness and the stillness
Bathing myself in the sickness and illness
Handcuffing myself to torment and anguish
If I don't all but die, I'll continue this languish

Dreaming of those tears falling, as I smile
I've been wanting you for quite a while...

Hello There

Hello there
How have you been?
It's so good
To see you again

Hi there
You look like you've been well
Although I know,
You've been through hell

Greetings my love
What should we do?
Been forever
Since I've seen you

Hello my dear
Shall we share a kiss?
It's been so long
But it's not the only thing I missed

Hi gorgeous
Would you like a drink?
Seems like you'll disappear
As soon as I blink

Goodbye my love
Seems like you just got here
But I knew when I blinked
You'd disappear

Helping Hand

By: Great Grandpa William Weatherhead

Young men don't like this filthy war
They have to fight and die.
While you and me here at home
Are living fast and high.

Let's get our shoulder to the wheel,
And give a helping hand.
These boys are only human;
Be they black, white, or tan.

For they are all good fighters,
That come from this free land.
So put your shoulder to the wheel,
And give a helping hand.

For they are really in the mud
In this far of place.
Let's keep America clean and free
And it won't be a disgrace.

Keep Old Glory flying high,
Here and over there;
And pray the war is over
Before another year.

I Am Here

He's almost here
I can feel it
Just like tomorrow
I want and need it
With out him
I choke
And I cannot breathe
And with out him
I am not sure
How to be me

He's on his way
Just another day
Then another one
Then a few more
And then
I'll watch him step off the airplane
And through the door
And I'll kiss his lips
And make him melt
And make sure
It's the best thing
He's ever felt

And I'll whisper in his ear
That I am here
And there is nothing in the world
That he should fear
And I'll tell him I love him
And how much I missed him
And how fucking horrible
These 9 months have been
And how much I cried
And every time I tried
To tell him how I was
I flat out lied
And said I was doing ok
But he knew better anyway
Because he knows I can't
Stand being away from him
For one God damn day

Then he'll wipe away my tears
And whisper that he's here
And tell me that there's nothing in the world
That I should fear.

I Could

I could scream to the great Goddess Venus
And still no one else would hear me
I could stare into the suns' eyes
And still no one else would see me
I could run to every ocean
And still no one else would drive me
I could scratch the sky and make the stars fall
And still no one else would know me

But I could whisper your name
Just once, to the night
And still you would hear me
As if I were in plain sight
I could touch my body
And still you would feel me
I could cry to my pillow
And still you could comfort me

14 hours, 1,000 miles, driving 1 whole day
But in my room thinking about you
You'd feel me just the same

I Feel

I feel as though my legs are amputated if I walk too long

Because when you're gone, I'm not that strong

I feel like my vision goes blurry when I

am awake for too many hours

Because when you're gone I'm with out my powers

I feel as if my heart stops beating

when I don't hear your voice

Because when you're gone, I know I don't have a choice

I feel useless when you're away

So just please fucking come back today

I Hate You 2009

2009 you greedy bitch
You made me cry and made me itch
You sent that bus that pulled up and took him away
Said he would return on the 365th day
2009 you're a dirty whore
You sent the person I love the most, right off to war
You stole my tears every night
Made everything go wrong when it was going right
You made my son ask, "where is daddy?"
And made him wonder, "Why did he leave me?"
I'll never forgive you two-thousand and nine
For being selfish and taking what was mine

I had him on New Years Eve
For the past 6 years
No pain, no loneliness, not one fucking tear

Now since you took him away
Going into 2010
I'll have to be alone again

I hate you and never want you back again, 2009
For taking what was rightfully mine
2010 will give him back
And there's not a DAMN thing, you can do about that...

21

I Hear Him Saying

I need a Bloody Mary to help me sleep
I don't think that makes me weak

And I hear him saying:
Dream sweet things my dear
When you lay your head down to escape the fear
Don't blame yourself for the things you do
We're all sinners too...

Then I slip into sub consciousness
Into a world of horrific manifest

And I hear him saying:
Don't worry about the demons dear
Nothing will happen when I am near
I'll fight them off one by won
Until the battle has been done

But I wake up on this couch, to an empty room
Laying in my self-made tomb

And I hear him saying:

Don't let my memory fade away

I'll be back some sunny day

When the demons haunt you, remember this

You're the only one, that I miss

And I smile inside as the monsters disappear

As I hear him saying:

I love you dear. . .

I Hope

I hope when you come
I get all my questions answered
I hope when you come
I'm not scared
I hope I can ask you
Everything I've ever wanted to
Do you love me?
Do you care?
Do you see us going somewhere?
I hope you can answer
All of these things
I don't want to wait
To see what the future brings
Will you kiss me?
Like you did before?
Will we repeat last time?
Or indulge in more?
You've been my secret desire
For over a year
Will I live that desire out?
Once you're here?
Please speak aloud
Tell me what you see
Then tell me the truth…

Do you love me?

I Reach the City

It's midnight under Northern Stars
And I'm missing you sincerely
Looking at open space
And wishing you were near me
Contemplating when I should come home to you
Wondering if there was anything else I could do
I wish it wasn't so hard and we didn't have to fall
Wondering if you miss me
Do you miss me at all?
Black and blue
As my heart aches for you
And I wonder how there was so much I never knew
A tear falls into the lake
And the moon looks sad; it's too much to take
I hop off the hood of my car
And say goodnight to my star
I start driving until its dawn and I reach the city
And when I see your face, it finally hit me
I can't live without you
I wouldn't want to
I'm in love as a fool
I guess that much I always knew

In This Dream

I wrapped myself up in a dream
And started to laugh instead of scream
I dreamt of things of me and you
And all the things I wish we could do

I tasted the wine of your sugar lips
And your hands of gold washed over my silver hips
Then you told me that diamonds couldn't compare to my eyes
Did I ever tell you your voice makes the angels cry?

You whispered to me in words of velvet
And told me things I'll never forget
Then I spoke back softly things into your ear
And took away all of your fears

In this dream that I had dreamt
I took back all the things I never meant
I took them back so quickly so easy
Because none of that means anything to me

I think of things I wish we could do, like maybe make love on mars
And find ourselves living among the stars
We'd put things like magic and miracles to shame
Because it's sweeter than that when you speak my name

In this dream I think a lot of things through
In this dream, at least I have you

Just a Dream

I thought I felt you yesterday but realized it was just a dream
Nothing with out you is as good as it seems...

I can't let this happen, this can't be real
I wake every morning to wounds I can not heal
When did this happen, where did it start?
When did God decide we should be ripped apart?

I look at the people, going about there lives
Wondering if they've been stripped
from their kids or their wives
I think, "I bleed, I laugh, I cry just like you"
"So why isn't this something you're going through?"
How were we chosen, how did he pick?
Sometimes not knowing just makes me sick

I close my eyes and think of how you felt
How in one word or stare, you could make me melt
And how we've been together now, for quite awhile
But even with a touch, you still make me smile

I thought I saw you yesterday but realized it was just a dream
Nothing with out you is as good as it seems...

Lie, Cheat, Steal, & Kill

The thought of you leaving tears me in two
Does it do anything to you?
We've done our time apart
No one knows how it weakened my heart

Laying numb, torn, and ill
I'd do anything to keep you here
I'd lie, cheat, steal, and kill

When you're away, you take all of my soul
It takes an unbearable toll

Call me crazy but I'd stop breathing without you
I'll try to make it but I'll struggle
the whole way through

They can tell me I can live without you
But what do they know?
What would you say if I asked you not to go???

Magic in the Snow

There's magic in the snow
As it melts today
It means winter
Could no longer stay
It means spring is coming-
And coming soon
It means no more of those-
Lonely afternoons

There's magic in the snow
As it fades to puddles of water
It's a sign of him returning-
And my nights getting hotter
It means kisses of cherry-
And watermelon
It means laughter and touching
And story tellin'

There's magic in the snow
As it fades away
It means he's coming soon-
Although it's not today
It means no more seasons alone
The start of something new
It means spring is coming-
And so are you. . .

Master of Time

I'm a fool for not trusting
But fear runs through me like floss
Doubt showers me
And the rain clouds swarm above forever
Nervousness, a sign of weakness
And I hate myself for being
So scared of what I should trust
My body is calm but in my head
Chaos is striking up a war
No one would ever be able to tell though
I hide it too well, but not from myself
The person I want to fool is me
But that won't happen
For I am a coward in my own eyes
Self-defeat shall eat me alive
And spit me out into the Black Sea
I consider myself a dreamer
A believer in fate
But I cannot help but hate myself
For obviously being fake
Time isn't so long to wait
But I just can't help being impatient
After all, I have waited a long while
But you see, there I go again
Saying what I've done
And not what you or God have done for me
And I cannot help but feel helpless
And nothing compared to you

I am sick of being drenched by doubt
The clock ticks…and I break it
Think I can master or rule time
But I cannot, for I am not God
But either are you, and still
I feel like you are the Ruler of Time
Controlling it just right, so I go insane
Wanting you more but I only doubt you
I am selfish for believing in my love for you
But questioning you and your own everlasting truth
It's not so hard to sit and wait
But it's hard to soak
In a bath of cowardness
For I begin to hate what I've become
For the time being that you
Are on your way to see me

Motels

Pitch dark – Super 8
Door to outside – late December date
Inside – bodies move
A reunion – in the mood
How long – will this go on?
Won't know – until I'm gone

A relationship – consisting of traveling
Closed doors – clothes unraveling
Fast food – airplanes
Motels – am track trains

A time difference – four states
A cycle – few relate
Long distance calls – lonely halls
Both looking at opposite sides of the moon
Praying to see each other soon

Numb

Voices surround and my head swirls into numbness
The sounds become distance and hollow
I get strange glares and stares as though I'm a ghost
Or perhaps, I look to them as though I've seen one
When I'm happiest in this world
Is when it hurts to be away from you the most
It's a constant reminder of the emptiness my heart carries with out you near
And the dagger that drives through me reminds me
you not returning is my constant fear
My legs feel amputated when I walk for too long
With out you near me, I'm not very strong

When my eyes are open all I see is fiction
A fairy world where nothing I do really matters with out you
As though my actions and words mean little to everyone around me
I think you're the only person that I mean number one to
And it's hard to know I don't truly matter to anyone
else but the one who's a half a world away
So I try to find you and see you in the eyes of strangers every single day
Funny how distance to many, is seen as an obstacle
But to me it makes me realize how strong we are together, and helps us grow

When I'm happiest I miss you the most and then some
So until you're in my arms again, my heart will remain numb...

Only the Strong

Only the strong survive...

Familiar, cheap, hotel room suites
Smoky halls, long – distance calls
14-hour drives

Only the strong survive...

Midnight losses of breath
Feels like an addiction to meth
Missing each other so badly at times
Hard to be happy just to be alive

Only the strong survive...

Weekends when every second matters
When Sunday comes, all dreams shatter
Just together, now the countdown starts
Again at day one hundred and five...

Only the strong survive...

Our Fighting Lands
By: Great Grandpa William Weatherhead

The boys leave their happy homes
And all good things behind.
While you and me are out to get,
All the pleasure we can find.
These boys are only human
Each and everyone.
And they are not over there,
Just to have some fun.

We run and gallop and whoop it up,
We are always on the "run".
While the boys are in Viet Nam,
Each packing a heavy gun.
These lads left their happy homes,
Each and everyone.
And they are not over there,
Just to have some fun.

Let's you and me in this free land,
Give this filthy war a think.
It is not a plaything for the boys,
To them it really stinks.
They are fighting in this far-off place,

Each and everyone.
And they are not there for their health
Or just to have some fun.

This war is not picnic for any human being,
To all it is the most corrupt
Man has ever seen.
The boys are fighting in Viet Nam
Each and everyone.
And they are not in Viet Nam
Just to have some fun.

Let's face the war like heroes,
With blood and bitter tears.
And pray the war will be over
Before another year.
We are in this U.S.A.
To help these fighting lads,
Put our shoulder to the wheel
And we'll be thankful for what we had.
Remember all in the U.S.A.
And all under the sun
These boys are not in Viet Nam
Just to have some fun.

Our Men in Viet Nam
By: Great Grandpa William Weatherhead

Sometime I'll write a little poem
As good as I can.
And if I'm wrong, correct me.
It's about Viet Nam.

Our men are there in force,
Black, white, and tan;
All are there for one thing,
To win in Viet Nam.

This war is dirty for any race,
Be they black, white, or tan.
All are there to
Win in old Viet Nam.

Our men are dying over there
In this far-off place.
And 'tis no pleasure to die in war,
No matter what the race.

Home people take it easy
But do keep up the pace.
So our men will have a place to come,
Not matter what the race.

Stick by President Johnson
Black, white, and all.
Do not let our men down,
Or we are headed for a fall.

Go to church on Sunday,
Pray for one and all.
Hope some day we'll meet again
If we live to tell it all....

Paradise without You

So, here I am underneath paradise skies
Swimming in Hawaiian air
Somehow, I just don't care
The ocean goes for miles
Got a little closer to heaven on the mountain today
But without you, it's just not the same

Paradise without you
Is like a ghetto without booze
The stars aren't as bright
And somehow, day is night
Bellowing, I call for you
Stormy weather, gray skies, no blue

The air isn't quite as sweet
Your presence is almost impossible to beat
Constant remembrance of you
So why do I do what I do...?

Reunited

An old flame
A faded name
A familiar sidewalk
A nervous shock

*

The Milky Way
A faded day
A year and a half missing
The two of us not kissing

*

A new fire
A burning desire
A long lost kiss
Oh! Sweet bliss!

*

My heart melts into yours
You say you haven't felt this before
We have to part once again
But in a year and a half it will be like we've never been

Sun and Moon

For months now I've watched each second on the clock pass
Waiting, wondering, how long this torture will last
Each day a reunion getting closer that will mend our souls
I'll wait for you until I'm gray and old

My body is constantly numb and cold
Shaky and uneasy, this never gets old
It's a good kind of pain
Like a bruise you wear like a badge, or a scar that tells a story
The bloodier the better
I like the hurt
I love the glory

Waiting, watching, anticipating
Hating not knowing, what this could bring...
But in the end it's all the same
This thing called life seems more like a game

Time drags on and on as though it knows I don't want it to
Like it knows all I want in life is you
Each second hurts and annoys, like water dripping out of a leaky faucet
The prize goes to the one who really wants it
And I want you, that's all I really know
I'll wait for you, until I'm gray and old

And although all this is true and, forever, I'd wait for you
I don't really want it to take that long, I don't really want to
So come home safe and come home soon
And we'll be waiting. . .
Him, your sun and I, your moon.

The Call of Duty

The call of duty is upon us
And I crumble to my knees
The buses pull up to get you
And I beg of you please

Take it all back
And forget all of this
Tell me things won't change
That there will be nothing to miss

A hug for our son
A kiss for me
Then you board the bus
And I watch until I can no longer see

One month passes...
Two
Three
Four
Praying everyday
I won't get that knock on my door

Five then six
Soon seven then eight
And no one I love,
Can even relate

One day it'll be twelve
And you'll back here with me
A kiss for our son
And hugs for the whole family

And as much pain as we've all endured
It was worth it as you break free from the crowd
Because you honored our country
and defended our freedom
And you've made all of us proud

The End

Setting out before the sun comes up
I hope that the weather will have some good luck
Early morning coffee
My radio playing quietly
Now the sun is starting to join me
And the birds are singing sweetly
Soon I'll be crossing the state line
With nothing but you on my mind
I have ten more hours to go
Time is going by so slow
A raindrop falls in front of me
And the sun hides as it starts pouring
I stop to fill up on gas
Hoping this storm doesn't last
Funny how this morning I was worlds away from you
Now this trip is half way through
Passing yet another state line
With nothing but you on my mind
I stop at a small café
I grab some food and get on my way
The sun is now getting tired
And has to light the other half of the world
My headlights cut through the night
And I'll be with you soon
I didn't think I'd cry but now I just might
I see a sign that says 'Happiness: 20 Miles Ahead'
That's the sweetest thing I've ever read
I see your car instantly
And scream in spite of me
Without even knowing when or how
We're safely inside kissing
And the worst is over now!

The Nights Are Darker

The day has been so long
Trying to fill the time and space while you are gone
Every second filled with you
It's hard to know what to do
Surrounded by strangers, dangers, and fears
Spending all my time, wishing you were here
A war between my heart and head
While my body tells me to go to bed
The breeze and warmth wash over my body
As I lay wondering what you're doing without me
The sun is not so yellow, the sky not so blue
But the nights are sure darker with out you

The Past 9 Months

Day 1:
All hope was lost
springtime,
I prayed for the frost

Day 30:
Only a month had passed?
The whole year
would this pain last?

Day 42:
Worse than the day before
Crying silently
Unable to take more

Day 62:
Saw his face again
Day 66:
It all ended too quick

Day 67:
No end in sight
Feeling hopeless
A useless fight

Day 83:
Not feeling any better
Only good thing?
The weather

Day 140:
The days pass like syrup
Struggling
this needs to hurry up

Day 164:
The leaves change colors
I pray
I am a good enough mother

Day 188:
Our 1 year anniversary
How I spent it?
In complete misery

Days 189 thru 218:
Horrific
Loneliness like you've never seen

Day 219:
Thanksgiving?
While he's away
I'm not even living. . .

Day 256:
Happy New Year
Resolution?
To escape the fear

Day 276:
I sit here waiting
Clock ticking
Contemplating

Day 276 still:
2 minutes have gone by
I wait
And try not to cry

Day 277:
It's almost here
My son's 3rd birthday
We escape our fears

He'll open presents and eat cake
But he won't need any rest
He's been waiting 9 months,
To play with the one present he'll like the best. . . . .

Twenty-One

By: Great Grandpa William Weatherhead

At the ripe old age of twenty
And maybe twenty-one.
I started to travel here and there
To try and have some fun.

I'd go on a tear on a Saturday night
And as sure as Old Ned, I'd get in a fight
Came in one morning, my head it felt light
Mama said, "Son, you were in another fight".

Mama said, "Son go get the mail
And don't forget, boy to wash the milk pail".
The letter that came, made a man pale,
For it came from Uncle Sam, 'twas stamp free mail.

Mama opened the letter — she let out a cry
She said, "My son, this will open your eye.
Read it boy, and read every word
This letter, my boy, is from the Draft Board".

My black eye stuck out, this is not fair
All my young plans blew up in mid-air.
Mama said, "Son, you're hooked by the draft
Don't worry, boy, this war just can't last".

I was sent to a Boot Camp, 'twas real far away
Me and all others were there for a stay.
They taught me good manners and also to fight
And I didn't go out on a Saturday night.

Come home on a furlough, before a cold spell
Wished Mama and all at home real well.
From now on I'll be flying real high
For I got me a job, with a Jet in the sky.
Next thing I knew I was a flying man
And was off in a hurry for old Vietnam.

When on my first mission,
'Twas a rugged old flight
I'd rather go out on a Saturday night.

Viet Nam

By: Great Grandpa William Weatherhead

Never did I see a time,
In my sixty-seven years
This war we have in Viet Nam
Would bring a man to tears.

People they are greedy
They act like hungry apes
They would like to skin a louse for its hide and tallow,
And get all that they can take.

They get in a car that is on the book.
Some don't act like a man
They forget about the war we have,
In Old Viet Nam.

If we would listen to the word of the Lord,
And also the good old Book;
We would not have all this trouble,
By taking the word of crooks.

So people sit down and think this over,
And do the little you can.
Put faith in the Lord and in crooks,
Help the men in Viet Nam

Waiting for My Angel

Sometimes I drown in the middle of an empty room
Feeling as though I've been gassed by a poisonous fume
Silence cuts through me
However, unbearable noises make me feel like I'm not free
When a racquet is constant through the day
I miss you more in every way
I am eating away from the inside out
Open the floodgates and let in the drought
Cry for the fire inside of me
Laugh for the desire of eternity
An anonymous addiction I'm trying to feed
A perfect prediction, feel the need
The Earth is wobbling, rolling around
For the galaxies I am searching, never are they found
The sun in your left palm, the moon in your right
Only you can control morning, only you control night
Morning is the warning of a breathless day
This expression is my confession that no one can say
I apply my mask in the daylight it hardens but doesn't crack
At night thinking of you it crumbles but the reality I lack
So far away from being with you, like eternity
Everyday purgatory, every night the same old story
People say this is life, but how can they tell?
While I'm waiting for an angel, my angel, I tell them this is hell

When He's Away

He's leaving her yet again
This is how it's always been
She cries as he reaches the door
Can't he give just a little more?
A kiss that's a little longer
A hug, a little stronger
An 'I love you' that actually feels real
A look into her eyes that could actually heal

A few phone calls while he's away
Would make it easier in every way
A note left under her pillow to find when she goes to bed
Would help ease her mind and settle her head

But he doesn't even understand her
And he hardly even tries
As much as she asks him...
As much as she cries...

Where Is My Daddy?

Where is my daddy?
Where did he go?
Him being gone is the only thing I know

I see his face on this screen
What does this mean?
He's the coolest person I've ever seen

I wish he could play with me
Maybe wrestle around
Come in the door and tickle me to the ground

Where is my daddy?
Where did he go?
I miss him so much, more than they know

He looks so cool, brave, and strong
Mommy keeps telling me I'll see him again,
She says it won't be long

I can't make sense of all of this,
But she says it'll be okay
I'll just have to trust her when she says,
He'll be back for good some day. . .

Craziness & Creatures

"It starts with the thoughts that flow through my brain.
Creating wicked stories that will drive you insane." -CCV

4 Course Meal

Sitting in this dark room
Suffocating on the fumes
Eating the doom
With a fork and a spoon

Put some salt on this hate
Add some desperation to my plate
God I can t wait
To eat up all the people, that can t relate

Add some sugar and spice
And nothing that s nice
Mix some depression with rice
And pour some blood over ice

No you can t join, cuz I locked the door
I d leave less for you and give me more
And I lay here bleeding, I eat on the floor
And get up, to go fill up, at the General s Store

Buy some milk and some skin
And a gallon of sloe gin
And the cashier says   Ma am,
you re looking quite thin
So I knock him out with his damn violin

Just give me a bag, make it paper not plastic
Sorry I won t smile today, I m not
feeling very enthusiastic
So I say to the stranger that I meet on the
street,   isn t life just so fantastic
When he agrees I trip the dumb ass for
not knowing I was being sarcastic

So I m back in my room
Suffocating on the fumes
Eating the doom
With a fork and a spoon

I m quite content here
All alone with my fear
Drowning in beers
And all my black tears

I won t be apologetic
For being unsympathetic
I d rather be fucking psycho and poetic
Than like you, and so God damn pathetic

And you say I m crazy?
Amazing.
I say you re fucking shady.
Good, I hope you hate me

I just ate your happiness for dessert
I swallowed your heart and poisoned you with hurt
I ll take your luck and your shoes
but you keep your shirt
I ll finish off my meal with your smile and some dirt

Oh really? What s that you say?
You think I m crazy?
Wow,
Why don t you tell me something
that ll actually amaze me.

7 Deadly Sins

Sitting here feeling like I could drown
My head spinning round and round
I have to get ready for dinner soon
I better get up or the roasted flesh will be ruined
7 perfectly disgusting place settings
But whenever I try and set down number 8, it goes missing...
I wouldn't want to upset Mrs. Gluttony
She hates when there's not enough food for her disgusting belly
I hope I made enough eyeballs for Princess Envy
She likes them so much, the more she has, the more she sees
I pray Dr. Greed doesn't get mad
If his hearts and spleens taste sort of bland
I tried my best and I really slaved
I even decorated this fucking cave
I got a personal waiter for Mr. Sloth
He's so fucking helpless he can't even lift his cloth
Not even to wipe his face
Fuck, he's such a damn disgrace
Ms. Lust will be upset if I didn't boil the lips just right
I don't get it? She wants them fried to a crisp but still Red and Bright...
Oh great, all the blood for Sir Anger isn't chilled just yet
He's gunna throw a fucking fit, I bet
He won't be able to get buzzed in the first hour
So his fucking mood is gunna get sour
Then King Pride is gunna act all fucking mighty
Like, "Oh, I just KNEW it was gunna be this kind of party"

Oh really?
You knew did you?
Let's see how much better you could do?
Having all the deadly sins at your place for dinner
I know I'm not a saint but I'm not THAT good of a sinner
I hear them coming in the cave, already?
I hold my hands out...not even KIND OF steady
I fast forward to dinner when I sit there eating
Hoping they're all liking their food that's bleeding
Me and all my 7 best friends
Gee, I'm so glad I have them
All the sudden the door bell rings
Always count on unexpected things
Who the hell could it be, I wasn't expecting anyone else
As my roommate walks into my empty apartment she says,
"Aww, honey, you really shouldn't eat by yourself...."

A Story of a Faceless Girl

My face fell off today
Then it just got up and ran away
I don t know where it went
Then it said it had someplace to go,
not sure what that meant

I don t know if I want it back
It wasn t really my favorite
But the shitty thing is now I can t breathe
So I don t if I m awake or asleep

I wonder where the damn thing went...
Just shot my whole day to heck
I had shit to get done but I can t go out like this
A faceless girl will even make the dogs hiss

Well it s the next day and I went
out last night, faceless
Wow, people sure do get worried when
you re all flesh & making a mess
Walked into the bar with some
muscle, bone, and tissue
Everyone looked at me like, dude, what s your issue?

But what they don t know is what they don t see
Is the girl who s the real me
Only he knows who I am and can
really be sure I m real
And until he comes back, I m not allowed to feel

The little girl at the grocery store
screamed and called me a freak
And all the old ladies in the coffee
shop let out quite a shriek
The guy at the clothing store yelled at me
because I was getting blood everywhere
Man, when your face is ripped
off people sure do stare

I had an itch and when I scratched
it some flesh fell off
And some old man just did the AH-
HEM, look at the weirdo   cough
People really don t approve of
this whole faceless thing
They whisper and they laugh and they
call the cops and they scream
I ll save my love, my effort, and my kisses
And bottle up the things that I know he most misses
Then I ll put them in a jar or maybe a big box
And tie it in bows with ribbons and knots

So I think my face ran off to find him
Tell him how hard this has been...
I ll get a package ready tonight
But when I m done I ll be quite the sight

I ll pack up most of my hair and rip off all my nails
So I ll be bald and bleeding from my cuticles
I ll make an incision and cut out my
hipbones and my lower back
Because I know he really misses that

Then I ll take my breasts and my stomach too
Bottle them up so he says, this feels just like you
Then I ll remove my eyes so I m
left with empty sockets
Next I ll take out my tongue so my
mouth is a hollow pocket

My voice box will have to be removed as well
And when I m done, I ll look like I belong in hell
I ll walk around this way until he comes back
And he brings home all the bits and
pieces of me in one big sack

People, sure they ll be frightened and
hate me... but hey what s new?
Nothing means anything, with out you...
I m empty and lifeless and hollow while he s gone
But my heart is not broken yet...so
don t you dare say I m not strong

And I Cried

Surrounded by confusion
Dismay, heartache, and pride
I sat in my room all Sunday and cried
Cried because I lied
Cried because I tried
Cried because a huge part of me has died

I swing at the emotions
With fists of steel
I would be overjoyed
If none of this were real

The monsters came out
From underneath my bed
And sank their claws
Into the part of me that's dead

The emotions are more alive than the monsters in my room
I should see a sunny future
But I only see doom

And I cried on Sunday
Cried because I lied
Cried because I tried
Cried because a huge part of me has died

As She Drinks His Red Wine

Its sick in the way it walks

Like poison as it talks

One of those things like an axe through the brain

Creating stories that'll drive you insane

Straight jackets and padded walls

Thunder roaring as the rain falls

And it goes crazier with each fallen drop

And every second that moves on the clock

And in its mind it's going bezerk

Thinking of ways to stop the hurt

Her nails grow with each full moon

She'll be out of this jacket sooner than soon

They don't know the things she hides

As she takes all of the torture, in full stride

Slowly clawing at the fabric that's bound her for years

She watches the days pass as she fights back the tears

Bloodshot eyes through the black cores

She tilts her head back and they hear her roars

Making the thunder now sound so much weaker

She breaks through the walls and runs into the forest deeper

Her skin like white wine and just as sweet

It's hotter now, in the summer heat

Night falls upon her and covers her up

As she drinks his red wine, from a cup. . .

Because of you

If you walked into my room
This is what you'd see
Me lying numb, mindless
And bleeding

One eye rolled back
To the back of my head
You'd think I was,
But I'm really not dead

The other eye staring
Straight at you
Look at this mess
Look at what you made me do

You'd see gashes here and there
And some things black and blue
And you'd wonder why
But it's all because of you

You think you've helped
But you haven't at all
You think you tried
But you barely ever call

I suffocate most days
And I give up trying to breathe
It's pointless to try and feel
When you always seem to hurt me

My heart is on my sleeve
I know you can see it
It's that thing that looks like a rotten tomato
Can you believe it?

It's just hanging there
Barely by a thread
Just about dried out
From being overly bled

My knees are all bruised
From begging for you
I thought when you loved someone
That's something you didn't have to do

Your thoughts are so ignorant lately
Your open-mindedness, a blur
Can you for once just not be so naive
And let insanity occur?

My skull is sort of bopping around
Like one of those bobble heads
And yes, it because of you
Please don't blame the meds

Yes I like beer
And I like to party
I like doing some crazy things
But how could you judge me?

When it's all said and done
Ask yourself what you did or how hard you've tried
Did you even notice
How much I cried? ....

Blood Bath Love Story

I walked down the dark street
and I swear a saw a boy
I saw him in the summer heat on
the corner of Main and Leroy
As I drew closer he coward away from me
He was not a boy and not a man
and nothing in between
His eyes were black and his skin pure white
And lips so red and bright
His nails were sharp and his hair was dirty
And I swear when he saw me, he
looked right through me

Like a horror movie type of love song
We met and it wasn t long
Until I became him and he became me
In this dark fantasy blood bath love story

I walked towards this thing and he shuttered
Don t come a step closer,   he muttered
I saw you and I love you and I
don t want to kill you
I asked him,   You won t really hurt me, will you?

Like a horror movie type of love song
We met and it wasn t long
Until I became him and he became me
In this dark fantasy blood bath love story

Then the pack came thundering down the alley
Faster than ever before
I have to hurt you to save you,
or they ll hurt you more
I told him okay
And he whisked me away
To a place I ve never seen
A place that I couldn t even find in my dreams
I tried not to cry
But it hurt so bad I thought I could die

Like a horror movie type of love song
We met and it wasn t long
Until I became him and he became me
In this dark fantasy blood bath love story

There we were, both now the same
In love and together and I didn t
even know his name
He smiled at me and reached for my hand
Come with me to my foreign land
I felt up to the two holes now in my neck
Smiled and thought.... oh, what the heck...

Bloody Fingers

I run down my fingers
Til they bleed
Taking things
I barely need
Raw finger tips
And warted skin
Reminds of places
I shouldn t have been
They re hard and callous
And chipped and cracked
I have no idea
How to quite react
I pinch them together
They stick and they swell
They look like the fingers
From the Devil s Hell
The bones are broken
Dislocated and popped
The noise so disturbing
I cover it up with a fit of coughs
My thumb is missing
Where did it go?
Ran away to someone better

This I know
My palms are maps
Of places I ve been
Some I want to return to
Some never again
The lines read like roads
The scars read like a nightmare
The burns and the cuts
Remind me that life is unfair
So I take a machete
And chop of my left hand
But I ll keep my right,
To catch me if I fall, before I land...

Creature

I look in the mirror and see my eyes are hollowed out
And my lips are sewn together
It is a disturbing sight
To see this horrific creature that is I
I am a lost cause and I hate it
If I were truly a human being I would tell you how I feel
And see what you see
I am naked, wrinkled to my bones
And decaying as seconds pass
Being fake for so many years
Has taken its toll on my body
I resent only myself for these results
My soul doesn't know
Where it should go
I look like a monster from the underworld
Hell is not a place to live
Angels glare at me
Devils sneer and curse me
Where do I belong?
Me, the creature I am I decide to end this so-called life
I crawl to the tallest building
And prepare to fall into the ground
Maybe further if that is fate
I take a step that is not there
And fall into the sky
When I open my eyes, I see clouds
And realize I am flying
God has saved me after all
I am worthy and now I can fly
I am beautiful and I am flying
Bliss! Joy is mine!
Happiness is this!

Crimson Illusions

Its starting to wear on me
Like a bad scar
Infected and itching
Bleeding through the scabs
Pussing through the stitching

First its on my forehead
I look down at my cards
Pocket Aces
Covered in blood
I feel my skin
Nothing is there

Next its my neck
I lift my hair up
Its soaked in thick red cranberry sauce
The smell sweet and rich
Grazing my fingers upon my collar line
I feel nothing

Then its my chest
My torso
They give me hugs when I enter the bar
When they pull away,
They're covered in blood
Her white fur coat, sprayed ruby red
His sharp new t-shirt
Stained
I look down and see nothing
Feel nothing

Then my knees
I crawl on them
Playing with him
Farm animals and trains
The carpet splattered with red finger paint
I yell at him,
but it is me
My knees
They are dragging the blood around,
like a paintbrush
I frantically look to my ruined jeans
But they're perfectly in tact

My feet
I take off my boots at the party
The entryway, nice and tidy
I hear a sloshing in them
I dump them out
The blood spills out
Like apple red paint
from a paint can
But my toes are still fine
Painted a dull blue from 2 weeks ago

I go home and undress
The mirror shows a smooth body
Scarless
Scabless
Ivory and firm

But the floor is covered in blood
I slip on it
Falling to the floor
I keep falling
Further
Further into nothingness

A weightless feeling over comes me
Like flying, but not as pleasurable
Just as I start to really panic
Just as I start to flail
Just as dread overcomes me
As I'm about to scream
As I'm about to lose my breath and lose my mind
Just as I'm about to die
✘
✘

I wake up,
✘
✘

Damn Sheep

Running.
Tryin' to think of something
Tryin' to yell or maybe just shout
Ugh, I don't even know what I'm mumblin' about

I just have this jingle jangle in my head
It's fuckin' noisy
So I can't get to bed

Yip Yip
Yap Yap
Rip Rip
Tap Tap
See....???
How do you get rid of THAT???

Sheep one....two......2,309
I'm on Cloud 5...
I need a map to Cloud 9

Hmmm I'll ask that guy, he looks like he knows
He might have a map I suppose...

Oh, right...this isn't real...
I forgot that I was typing this in bed
What's my fucking deal?

I don't even know what's going on
I think something's seriously wrong

Shit I've already counted 5,000 of these creepy looking sheep
I thought this was supposed to help me sleep?

Some people take Ambien...
But nah, I'm just gunna keep ramblin'

Are you actually reading this???
haha, hope you're enjoying my bullshit...

So, how are you? Did you have a good day?
We should probably hang out soon, what do you say?

Roseanne is on...it's pretty funny, although I have it on mute
But Jackie's little black dress is really cute...
I think my hands are cramping but I can't really tell
I think my eyes are bloodshot but oh well

What's that you say?..I'm crazy?
Wow, really?? Why don't you tell me something
that'll actually amaze me...

Duh, most people would just at least talk to themselves
But nope, I'm gunna type and act like
I'm surrounded by elves...
Why?
Oh, I don't know...
Maybe it has something to do with the snow...

Oh man, you shoulda seen it...
That fat sheep just tripped over the fence
NO, I MEAN IT...
Oh......I actually think he might be hurt...
Face planted right in the dirt...
That shit was funny though
Ok I'm gunna go

I think I bored myself enough just now...
Gunna go watch this muscle-y sheep fight that huge cow

Wow, congratulations if you'd made it this far...
This is getting long and really boring...
Maybe you should be sleeping and dreaming and snoring

I think that I'll go get a cookie...
and ta

.

. .

.

Whoops I think I feel asleep...
Damn sheep

Deformed

My eyes have bruises
And my tongue is numb
My body is blood shot
I have black and blue lungs

I'm crying from my fingers
And I'm bleeding from my hair
I'm falling on this climb
And choking on air

I'm sinking when I'm floating
And I'm suffocating while I'm breathing
I think I'm outside in and downside up
Did I mention that I'm bleeding?

I'm blinking through this stare
And I am living through my death
I'm concentrating, unfocused
I'm down to my last breath

Who woulda known I could do this
We're almost to the end
I might be twisted by the time you get back
But a little rearranging and I'll be easy to mend

My knees are hollow from begging for you
And my skin is all but burnt
I don't look anything like the girl I used to be
Please take away the hurt

Don't they see this girl, she's dying
Can't they hear her screaming and crying?
I refuse not to live through my own death
Even if I am down, to my very last breath
...
I'll hold it until you get back
I'll be here mangled, deformed, and waiting for you,
IF you still want that. . .

Devil and the Demons

And the world keeps beating us down
Until we re lit with flames and we
fall through the ground
Fire and glass aren t even the start
But we ll keep swinging and fighting
until we re torn apart

I woke up today with a needle in my eye
I crossed my heart and started to lie
I guess some old wives tales really do come true
Now I have to drown with you

With the demons we ll put on
gowns and have a dance
And glance back on the days where we
should have got a second chance
I took at drink with the Devil because
he was the only one with whiskey
But I tried to run away when he got a little frisky

Fallen angels and tormented lost souls
They all act like they love you,
and act like they know
They clothe themselves in gold and lie
All the while, wishing you d die

Dante s inferno didn t do justice
To the things that the anti-Christ has planned for us
In the glimpse of my nightmares
I ve seen these bad fortunes
And have shuttered at the pictures
of the broken ones

And in these times where the world gets dark
Find those to are trustworthy and those who aren t
Try to tear back their masks and
their to-good-to-be-true deals
And find the ones you know are real

Never trust someone who wants to see you in heat
Someone who will relish in your defeat
Never trust someone with horns
or someone who loves red
I d rather die with someone who s lived
than to live with someone who s dead

Dollz

They wear pink and purple and ribbons and bows
I wear black from my eyes to my toes

They show off their diamonds and
pearls and silk and lace
I sport skulls, and revolvers, and the smokin ace

Their jeans cost 80 dollars, hell maybe even 200!
I wouldn t spend that much on clothes in
6 months wouldn t be caught dead!

My jeans have rips and holes and stains and creases
All my shirts are purposely torn to pieces

They get mani s and pedi s and
take time on their hair
I go out with my nails chipped and bare

I have tattoos and red streaks and
I curse like a trucker
And I am most definitely not like her!

I like poker and beer and shooting loud guns
We re a few and far between, they
call us the chosen ones

They smile 24/7 and laugh when they should
Do they ever get sick of being so good?

I NEVER smile and I laugh when I shouldn t
And if someone told me to be
more lady like, I couldn t

They re glitter and heels and perfume and malls
They re the perfect robotic Barbie Dolls

I m leather and rock -n- roll and a little bit crazy
At the end of the day, I m just me.

Elevator To Where?

I feel like my guts are rotting
I feel like the demons are plotting
I honestly don't feel well
On this elevator to hell

I pressed the up button
But it said "Wrong Way"
I said, 'I just wanted to go up for a visit'
It told me "Not Today"

The music wasn't like normal
It wasn't light and airy
It sounded like screaming and people dying
Mom help me, this is scary

The ride down wasn't fun
And I started to get hot
I felt as though my brains were fried
And my stomach would flat out rot

I started to cry
But no tears would come
I pinched myself
But I was numb

I screamed out loud
But couldn't breathe
I pressed "Escape"
But couldn't leave

I tried to wake up
But I wasn't asleep
I tried to turn this nightmare
Into a dream

I tried to remember what I did
But couldn't come up much
I tried to give myself a great big hug
But I was too hot to the touch

It stopped to a halt
And opened the doors
I saw lines and lines
Of sinners begging on all fours

There was a line I saw right away
It was labeled : "Checking In"
But it was empty, with no one in it
I guess no one had thought they sinned

The line I was looking at
Was way too long
It was labeled
"What The Fuck, I Did Nothing Wrong"

Guess there would be a lot of time
To think this over
Waiting in line
On fire and sober

Then I realized what was going on
I realized I was in hell for the things I coulda been doing
But I wouldn't do that, and couldn't do that
For everything I'd be ruining

Then my last hour started rewinding
And I was heading up not down
I was headed to that cloud in the sky
Instead of the hole in the ground

I could breathe so much better
And felt some crisp fresh air
I knew where I was headed
I'd know many people there

Some I haven't seen for ages
Some who I just lost
But it's not so sad after all
If you think of the real cost

I can't wait to see him
We wait our whole essentially for this!
When I see Jesus, I'll be so excited
I think I'll give him a kiss

Forgotten Ever After

I walked in and saw some flames and shards
Some pieces of glass, some soft, some hard
I saw some blood and some guitar picks too
For a second I kinda thought it was you

I saw some bones all broken and scattered
And an empty tube of lipstick that was completely shattered
I saw a shrunken skull and a pair of high heels
I wish I could go back to the day that none of this was real

I closed the door behind me and locked myself in
And got ready to drown with the sorrow of my sins
I sat on the chair that was made of nails and needles
And grabbed a fork for my dinner of snails and beetles

I didn't have regrets till I entered this room
But now I know that it has led to this doom
I looked in a cracked mirror and saw my hair disappear
And I saw all my dreams go down the drain like a vat of stale beer

Then I saw a case of liquor bottles, with a lock, with no key
And I realized I couldn't ever drink them
again, oh the torture and misery.
And then I saw the chocolates and smelled the sweet smell
And when I realized I couldn't eat them, I knew this was hell

Then the worst thing happened, I saw you- in a glass cage
And I ran at you with fire and passionate rage
I stopped to a sudden gasp when I realized you were frozen
And I'd have to burn in this inferno, for the things that I'd broken

Surrounded by all the things I loved and could no longer touch
I realized I had messed up just far too much
I just wish my heart would beat slower ... or faster
Instead, its beats have stopped for good, in my forgotten ever after....

Freak

I'm a freak
Are you too?
And if so which one are you?
Because there are so many types of freaks these days
It's not like it used to be used in a just one type of phrase
Now it can mean this
And it can mean that
It all depends on how you act

Are you freaky?
Like freaky deaky?
Like do you like to have sex and make it sneaky?
Do you like doing weird things sexually?
Like taping it and having people see?

Or are you the new age term and a regular freak
Hmm, that might be an oxy-moron I think
Oh well, you know what I mean
Like a freak who does weird things
Like swinging in the pool
And dressing like a fool
Or acting like you're on drugs
And giving kisses to strangers and enemies your hugs?

Or maybe you're the annoying freak
Who just uses the word in passing
Like "OH MY FREAKING GOOD THIS MOVIE IS A CLASSIC!"

Yeah those people are really annoying

And the ones who say "SERIOUSLY I AM FREAKING OUT"
What the fuck is that all about?

Or maybe you are the very first usage of the word?
Like how if you have a deformity you are considered absurd?
Do you have something wrong with your body or face?
If so then you're in the right place

Or perhaps you're a Freak Show
Ya know?
Like a Circus Freak
That's the best one I think
Because then you can be whoever you wanna be
And spend your life making people happy

And did you know there are other uses for the word freak?
Almost too many I think
Like describing mutations in animals in plants
Or saying "That's a freak of nature"
How about that?
And did you know that in the French or Scottish
heritage Freak can be used as a surname
It's not used often but isn't that insane?
And in a meaning through interpretation it's
seen as "Keeper of the Plains"
Again, isn't this shit just so insane?

So if you really think about it just for a second
You'll see something that you can relate to that I already mentioned
So in a way, if you really think
We're all just a bunch of fucking freaks!

FuCk It:

fuck fuck
damn damn
cans of coors
coors of cans

oh my God
oh my Lord
Peter Pan
Stone and the Sword

Or Sword and the Stone?
Or Who Gives a Fuck???
Yup I like that one
Now shut the fuck up

Am I angry
nah, why do you ask?
I think it's funny
Like laughing gas

That's messed up?
Is that what you said?
Well fuck you then
and you're stupid head

I enjoy it kinda
Just a lil' bit
You don't?
Well who gives a shit?

What's this about?
I mean really?
Who knows?
This poems getting silly

Now I think some stuff
Maybe I'm just writing to write
The grammars not even correct
Ah, FucK iT..............GoOd NighT....

Haunted

There is a ghost.... right outside my window
Whispering secrets of souls unbound
There is a spirit.... right out on my doorstep
Telling me of treasures unfound

And it s haunting me
It s taking me
It s torturing me to not know
And it s killing me
It s confusing me
It s burning into my soul...

There is a vampire... right next to my neck
He looks thirsty and uncontrolled
There is a man... on the other side of the room
He looks eager and alone

And it s haunting me
It s hurting me
It s killing me to not know
It s breaking me
It s bending me
It s burned right through my soul

There is a gypsy... dancing next to me
And she s sending me messages heart to heart
There is a zombie... bounding after me
Ready to tear me apart

And they re haunting me
They re stalking me
They re trying to tell me, so I know
They re helping me
And pushing me
To feed and nourish my soul...

These creatures, these emotions
They will never understand, they will never know
These creatures, these emotions
Are my words... my thoughts... my soul....

I have these dreams, or realities
Of being helped or being used
But it comes down to just some greater plan
It s easy to say I m confused....

In all of this, I think of the things I ve
needed and the things I have wanted
And realize how selfish I can be... it s
no wonder I m so haunted.

How He Played

His fingers were a little overweight
_____ But oh how he played~
A dusty fender
A candle lit to his room s background
_____ And oh the sound!
A face in such concentration
_____ But not quite meditation
His fingers were a little overweight
_____ But oh how he played~
~*~*~*~*~*~

Nothing like departure
Such appalling torture
Don t know exact words to say
Wasting time   slipping away
Looking down at you
From my bed
So many things I should have said
Who s to blame?
It just won t be the same...!
~*~*~*~*~*~

Close But no cigar
Or was it cigarette?
I guess sometimes I just forget
Just like you
Used to know all the right things to say
Now that I m here that just went away
~*~*~*~*~*~
My stomach is in knots
My arms; a drained sponge
Sweaty palms
And twitching leg
The disease is swimming
Through my veins
I ll finish this later...
I ll finish this later...
_____ But oh how he played~

I Woke Up This Morning

I woke up this morning and there
was this ringing in my head
Telling me to go back to bed
But what did I do?
I got up anyway
I got alotta shit to do today
So I went downstairs and what did I see
I saw a pack of wolves waiting for me
Ah shit maybe I ll go back upstairs
And no it s not cuz I m scared
Ya know, it s just that I really don t
feel like getting eaten alive
I d rather die a peaceful death if I died
Then I went up stairs and went back to bed
But when I woke up again there
was a buzzing in my head
I ignored it again cuz the wolves had to be gone
They couldn t really have waited
for me quite that long
So I skipped my happy ass downstairs
and what did I see
A posse of clowns with knives waiting for me
Ah shit maybe I should go back upstairs
And no it s not cuz I m scared
Ya know, it s just that I don t like
getting stabbed in the heart
At least not from them, hey, coming
from you, well that s the good part

Then I went back upstairs and went back to bed
But when I woke up there was this siren in my head
I shut it off and decided to try again
What other bad things could possible happen?
So I floated downstairs and what did I see
A vampire, a ghost, and an alien waiting for me
Ah shit maybe I ll just stay upstairs
And no it s not because I m scared
Ya know, it s just that I don t like getting
killed in three different ways
Maybe I ll just do my errands another day
So I went back upstairs and went back to bed
And I woke up with this song in my head
Fuck it; I m not falling for that, nope not this time
All of those demons had to be a sign

Two days later I woke up to silence
Yes, finally! I deserve this!
So I flew down the stairs and what did I see?
A note and dead flower waiting for me
I opened it up and read it out loud
And when I realized that I d missed
you I crumbled to the ground
I should ve listened to that fucking song
Now I m here alone and you are gone
I guess through all this, I learned something
To never, no matter the obstacles,
give up on your dreams
I should ve known to fight past the fear
Now you re miles away again, and I m stuck here

I'll Admit It

Let me think
Let me blink
A few times
Seems I'm running outta rhymes
Oh wait, I just did it
See, I knew not to quit it
It really only takes me a minute...
Now let's get started
Before this gets too retarded

I've been thinking so much lately but about crazy things
Weird, insane, memories
Things that make you go
WHAT DID YOU JUST SAY...
JORDAN?! ARE YOU OK?
Stuff that puts people away with the crazies
Like blackened, poisonous, blood covered daises
And pillows with skin in them filled with skulls
And feasting on hatred until you're full
Things like the sky raining acid
And turning your sweet smelling roses rancid
These things are strange and awkward
But who isn't a little absurd?
Geez and I thought I'd lost the ability to write
Well maybe someday, but not tonight...

Sometimes when I'm too happy I feel it slipping
But not right now when the pain is dripping

It seeps outta my body like lava out of a volcano
And spins inside my head like a F5 tornado
Illness in my soul and in my mind
But don't you worry about me,
I'll be fine
Maybe when he's back I'll leave you all alone
Put down the pen and paper and be normal at home
But until he's away I'll write everyday
And talk about things that most of you would never say
I'll admit I hate clowns and wish they would bleed
And I think we all WANT
More than we NEED
Everyone is selfish and everyone has sinned
And we all have probably wasted our time, more than we've lived
I'll admit I'll have a cocktail...or 3, alone at night
And I don't give a fuck if you think its right
I'll divulge that I loathe the color pink
Unless it's some blood draining down the sink
Also I think when someone makes fun of a red headed
step child, that it's something to laugh about
And if you don't like how messy my
room is then get the fuck out
And I bet you're thinking "Oh my God, you wanna
see an eyeball get stung by bees?!"
And I say "Yes, so if you don't like it,
then don't fucking read these"
And I'll confess I think about some other wacked up, scary shit
But I'll leave you alone now, leave it at this
I'll just end it by saying I MISS HIM
But if he wasn't gone, this poem would have never been...

InSaNe

I m a prisoner in this fucked up head
I can rarely get to bed
I think something s rotten up in there
It could just be like an ingrown hair
But I have the feeling its something more serious
Something s got me all delirious
I can feel something loose up in my brain
It s driving me fucking insane
I feel this little tick go tock
But I m pretty certain its not a clock
Its something up there that needs to be shut off
It s like the Devil s got a personal loft
Something is lurking in my brain
Its driving me fucking insane
I picture a little man or maybe a little girl
Up in there like it s there own little world
They have tools and machines and
some sort of torture device
I wish people would take their own advice
Shit there s that fucking ticking again
It goes tick tick tock in my mother fucking head
Its gunna go boom boom boom
Maybe bang bang bang
I like singing but its been so long since I ve sang
I like laughing but since when do I laugh?

I like driving but I don t got the gas
Maybe its all this poison in my brain
That s driving me fucking insane
Tick tick boom
Or tock tock tick
Fuck, I wish I was a normal chick
The countdown s on until he gets back
Then I m gunna kiss him like smack smack smack
I m gunna hold him until he makes the voices stop
He s really all that I got
I feel my brain starting to ooze
Maybe I should lay off the God damned booze
Its rotten up there I just know it, I can tell
I hope no one else can smell this smell
Maybe its just a little dusty, it could be mold
I m young in age but I feel fucking old
Tick tick tick
Tock tock tock
Where the hell is that fucking clock?
Shit now I gotta itch I can not scratch
Oh wait, that s just me wanting him back
I wish he wasn t so far away
But I m just glad it s not yesterday
There is something happening inside of my brain
That s driving me fucking insane
Guess I ll never know what it is
Looks like I m gunna have to live with this

-Men!

The trees blow severely

As the moon lights the stone and pathways

Unholy creatures and hellhounds stalk the dusk

Feeding off lifeblood of the innocent

From their deep beds they crawl out and prey

Pale corpses and nail like dentures

Demon like eyes with bloodlust

Taking naïve souls for their collection

They reek of arrogance

And maggots mixed in flesh

They feed off the succulent juices of the weak

These are terrible, villainous monsters

What are they-what is their title?

I think maybe ---

-Men!

Monster in Me

Something lives inside of me
A monster who is ugly and na ve
Creeping around, waiting to destroy my world
Tell me I m not a woman, and make me a girl
This creature is green and red
It has made me kill and has knocked me dead
Under fingertips and skin it lives
Waiting for me to crack and give
It s waiting to see me fall 1,000 feet
Waiting to spoil me until I stink of rotted meat
It burns at the core of my soul and heart
Waiting to slowly tear the goodness apart
It s laughing at me getting scared
It knows I ll just wait until I get dared
It feels the coward in me, the one who s afraid
The part of me that s lurking in the shade
The monster inside me is eating my guts
Because it knows I m not brave enough
I don t deserve to feel pride and respect
I want to but I m just a nervous wreck
Out of the bag, out of the box, out of my skin
The real me, is wearing thin
I act proud to people I don t know
But my monster knows I do this for show
I have to let it out, tell this creature to go away
But that would mean my coming out,
So I guess I ll do it some other day

Monstrous Justice or Beautiful Revenge?

Up in the attic in the eye of the storm
Another horrific and deadly creature was born
Years spent alone, feeling this yearning
Needing something, fighting this burning...
It scrolls through, trying to find an address or a name
In the books of the criminally insane
Nails scratching, the paper shredded
Feeling the thirst, becoming lightheaded
Starts in the blood stream and up the spine
Bones start cracking, as the crescent moon shines
A howl like something, but not quite evil
Dating back centuries, to something primeval
Blood now boiling and hair quickly sprouting
It takes off in the right direction, no time for rerouting
No longer needing a book or any help
Playing off the instincts it was rightfully dealt
Flying so fast through the forest and brush
Hunting and sniffing out, the sickly crush
Its beauty is so striking, it's just unspoken of
One glance at this creature and it becomes a deadly love
Piercing eyes and a soulful presence
Angels do not even hold an ounce of resemblance
The prey is now in the predators eyes
It's ready to kill the thing it's never loved, and always despised
Collecting the remains of the victims of many
Not stopping until it has gotten plenty
Bones and skulls and skulls and bones

Bottling up their screams and their moans
Keeping the terrified, painful voices
The creature's music is the sound of their excruciating noises
If this is getting too graphic, I'd stop here
But if not, listen close, and lend an ear
These creatures, they don't have mercy for the forsaken
Lives that deserve to be tortured and taken
Getting the fix from ripping them apart
Its wallpaper is the collection of their bleeding hearts
Sinners and haters and non-believers
Beaters and rapists and under-achievers
Accumulating their eyes, it took with its knives
And making them watch, for eternity, a replay, of their disgusting lives
Sealing up the tainted blood in vats upon vats
The creature hears the applause from the crows and the bats
They all wonder, what is this thing? Some sort of vigilante?
Either way, whatever it is, it's a beautiful monstrosity...

Museum Of Horror

They don't understand what they fear
And they fear what they don't understand
I'd like them to come visit me here
Take a walk, and hold my hand

See the world from the inside out
Open up their closed off brains
Try and see what this life is about
See the glory that comes from pain

They ask – what's that thing on your hand?
I say - oh this? ...Right here?
They say - yeah it looks like a wedding band
I say - I've only been wearing it, about a year

I tell them let us skip the happy talk
And get down and dirty
Get ready for a scary walk
I say, I hope you're not in a hurry...

We step into the Museum of Horror
And their mouths drop wide open
I say 'its ok I'm an experienced explorer'
But I don't know how well they're copin'

A beauty queen behind the glass
Who's scalp is crawling with worms
She just couldn't make the beauty last
Finally, her ego suffocated her

She sits in the chair
Half there, half not
No skin, no hair
She's starting to rot

Exhibit Two: A perfect male
Who's looks could almost kill
But his nose grew and he grew a tail
Now he's half dead and ill

His lies are tearing at his soul
His body all bled out
Surrounded by a bat and crow
He's turned into a monster with a snout

Behind door #3 I warn the crowd
This could get rather scary
Please bite your tongues, don't get too loud
Or it could get kind of hairy

Two creatures, one black, one white
Locked in their life long conquest
Neither giving up the fight
In the battle to see who earns highest prejudice

Tsk tsk, I shake my head
Such a bloody shame
If both continue this way, they'll end up dead
And both are fully to blame

We continue down the corridors
And I heard some vomiting and crying
We passed the pimps and the whores
All of them were dying

There were haters in the next room
Who hated, blacks, and Jews, and Gays
Living a torturous life of doom
For not accepting people these days

You could smell the decay
And the burnt hair too
I said the only thing I knew to say:
This doesn't have to happen to you

I've been there and I've done that
I know all the evils of the world
But right now I'm happy where I'm at
No longer, that fucked up girl

There's an easy fix and we all know it
Let's not get greedy, or we just might blow it

Temptations and evils, they come and go
But Thy Kingdom and Thy Glory: Forever
So let's not end up this way, in horror
Let's just handle each endeavor

Let there be no worms, or crows
Or bats
I don't want to end up a monster
Lets leave it at that.

I know this was long and I know it was rough
but thus ends the tour of the Museum of Horror
I just hope I have taught you enough
and don't forget to tip your 'Expert Explorer'

My Enemies

Time stole my laughter
And bottled it up
And then took my heart
And tore the shit up

Procrastination is not my friend
It killed my passion and drive
Took 'em out to the sand hills
And buried them alive

Jealousy is a bitch
She's a sad miserable woman
Wanting her looks and that voice
Not happy with what she's been given

Regret is annoying
It's a nagging old hag
Clawing at your emotions
Then stuffing them in a bag

Ignorance is useless
Stupid and callous and rude
I can be on cloud nine
And it'll put me in a mood

Arrogance is rotten
A power hungry whore
Always acting like he's something better
Always thinking he means more

Prejudice is a crime
Unwanted and pointless
Judging things it doesn't understand
Makes for quite the mess

I will never let anyone or anything make me feel hate
It is poison to the heart, mind, and soul
The list above are simply things I can not stand...
So at least now you know

107

Psychotic

Suffocating
Contemplating, going insane
It'd be easier if I didn't understand by brain
I'd just go psychotic
Hum things melodic
Talk to fruit and berries
Have imaginary friends
And pets that are fairies
Disown everyone I know
So I didn't have too feel this black hole
In it I swim and almost drown
I've spent too long
Crying on the ground
I just want to not feel
I'd rather be fake at this point,
Rather than real
Start pretending I don't care
That I don't cry
That I'm not scared
Get off my knees and beg no more
Open all of the windows
And fear the shut door
Just walk around yelling at people
And getting away with it
Saying all types of crazy shit
Just wear tube sock and underwear
Stop with make up and shave off my hair
Eat Spaghetti-o's outta the can

Come up with a way to take over the world
But not live out the plan
Sit on my rocking chair
On my roof
In the winter
Slide my hands down an old broken see-saw
Just for the feel of a splinter
Bark at small children as they pass
Chase after strangers
Just for a laugh
Sit on the floor and hug my knees
Rock back and forth
Repeating 'please'
I wish I were crazier
Than what I really am
Maybe all I need
Is a better plan
Just to not feel
SO FUCKING DEEPLY
This is my greatest wish. . .
Believe me.

Reflection

Look at that ugly girl, she disgusts me beyond belief
All she has for herself is pity and grief
It looks like she s never been loved
Even if she has, she was hurt
And it was just too much

Take one look at her it s revolting
She walks alone at night
She s a disturbing sight
What s her name? Who is she?
Was it love that tore her down or was it her destiny?

Is she lost or does she just not care?
She s stripped of everything, stripped, stripped bare
She ll never be a woman
Even when it s all took in

Everyone laughs at her
Maybe she s getting what she deserves
Ugliness has taken over her mind, body, and soul
It s about time she let go

Look at that girl she disgusts me beyond imagination
Looks like she s been sentenced
to eternal damnation

You need to get away from her
So you sit back and wonder why you re still here
You stand up suddenly
Break the glass before you and realize
The whole time that girl,
Was your own damn reflection in the mirror

Remind Me

Walked into the dungeon
I was having fun when
I saw it creep up on me
Maybe if I got some sleep lately
I wouldn't a been so scared
Not like I was actually dared
But I still felt dumb for running
I knew that monster was coming
Sneaking up right behind me
While the halls, they were winding
I tripped over a snake that tried to bite me
And saw a skull or two, well that was frightening
I fell in a vat of rats and mice
God, I could really use your advice
I slid down the sewer like a waterslide
Not so pleasant when it all collides
The smell burned my nose
I'd need a good shower from the hose
I ended up further in than out
Started to scream and started to shout
But the tarantula's shrieked right back at me
That is when I really started panicking
Eight legs are always worse than two
I had no idea what to do
So I sat down and rocked back and forth
Felt pain and loneliness and a bitter remorse
Just as I let the past go behind me
I realized you may forgive me, but these
creatures will always remind me

Scare the Monsters Away

I sit here alone and wonder why you're not here
Just me, my nightmares, and a case of beer
The monsters in the other room don't bother me much anymore
In fact, I think they've got so sick of my
crying, they've shut the door
And it's about time I get my act together one of these days
You know you're going crazy, when you
scare the monsters away. . .

I drive out here alone and get lost in
wishing you were here with me
Just me, my blood shot eyes, and a bottle of Hennessey
The monsters stalking the ditches don't worry me tonight
In fact, I think they've gotten so sick of the
swerving; they've given up the fight
And it's about time I get my act together one of these days
You know you're going crazy, when you
scare the monsters away. . .

I dance here alone in my living room, pretending I'm fine
Just me, this music, and a bottle of wine
The monsters surrounding me don't faze me right now
In fact, I think they've gotten so sick of my
moping, they've all scattered somehow
And it's about time I get my act together one of these days
I know I'm going crazy, because I scare the monsters away. . .

:sdrawkcaBBackwards:

My teeth are bleeding
And my nose is starting to decay
I down this glass of color
But the pain won't go away

My knuckles are falling out
And my hair is starting to crack
I stare at the clock
But you're still not back

My skin is starting to ache
And my bones are peeling
I down a few aspirin
But I still have this feeling

My guts are worn out
And my mind is rotten
I try and sleep the pain away
But your memory is not forgotten

But I know the day I see you, everything will be okay
My nose will bleed and my teeth will decay

I know I'll be normal again when you come back
My hair will fall out and my knuckles will crack

I just need you with me for God's sake
So my skin can peel and my bones can ache

I miss you, but it's not like I forgot
Because with out you my mind isn't worn out and my guts don't rot

Please, don't take this as a bad thing
This is the way life is SUPPOSED to be
So let's get back to some sort of normality

All of these things I can deal with in the right order
But when they're all scrambled and backwards, I can't take much more

So let us breathe together, and bleed, and love and cry
Come back soon, because with out you, I just might die...

I need you here to think and age
I need you for everything I do
All I know is that I'm lifeless and fucked up right now
Because I can't LIVE with out you....

Shadow

I have a friend who s really sad
Often lately she s been getting mad
It seems to me she s getting uglier
No one seems to be able to help her
She cries a lot and it hurts I think
To the point I m not sure she can blink
She yells a lot and punches walls
Never wants to answer anyone s calls
She gets pains a lot, mostly in her heart
And she says it feels like she s being ripped apart
She screams sometimes, until it hurts her throat
And she feels like she s drowning
instead of staying a float
She s bored a lot and really lonely
No one can help her, not even me
Time will help, maybe
Maybe not
She ll wait it out
It s her only shot
The people she loves are dropping like flies
Each time one leaves her, the harder she cries
She says the silence gets so loud
it almost hurts her ears
Then again so does the stinging of her tears
She stares a lot, into nothingness really
Most people think she just looks silly
I m talking to her now and people are staring
But neither one of us is really caring...

I wonder just how she got so low
Hello there, I d like you to meet my friend,
Her name is Shadow

115

She Watched Out Into the Darkness

Dull lamp lights lit the cobble stone
She while she waited, thirsty and alone
All the shops were closed and locked
But one would answer, if you only knocked

She waited there for a cocktail
Her hair black, her skin pale
She watched out into the darkness as they all passed
Wondering how long this dry spell would last

Then she saw him meandering alone
She smelt his scent and heard his bones
Her teeth got sharper and her growl got lower
He started walking- just a little slower

He looked a little lost and a tad bit confused
She turned on her store light as he sat on the curbside and mused
He looked up and she saw hope in his eyes
She wished she could love him, instead of being something she despised

Now he stood up and walked towards her for help
She wondered how loud he'd moan and he'd yelp
She didn't want to hurt him, poor soul didn't deserve it
But the thirst was taking over and she'd die if she didn't get it

They talked for hours, and again she fell in
love with another perfect boy
But she knew this love that would never
last was just a temporary decoy
She let a tear fall while he sipped on his warm cup of tea
Then she lunged for his neck, before he could see. . . . .

She-Wolf

Dark hollow trees
Still among the breeze
While the bloodhounds stalk secretly
In lands of infamy
Wanting blood and needing it
Feeling the hunger, then feeding it
Hunting those forbidden desires
Avoiding the hidden fires
Claws like daggers dig in the dirt
Pulling up the soil of the untouched Earth
Ripping up the nature and so much beauty
Doing it for the passion and the duty
Barely comparing life to this
A sweet scent of red, is the devils kiss
She's dressed in a gown on top of the hill
He's graining ground, ready to kill
The sky is dark and her dress is white
The coming of age, the sunset of night
His snout pulls back and reveals his fangs
And her shadow is cast by the moon, as it hangs
He leaps into the air, ready to get his fill
But she turns just in time, ready to kill

The Crow and the Bat
(Pt. I)

Wrong again said the crow to the bat
I know she loves you as a matter of fact
Just ask her yourself
You'll feel much better
Just the other day she sent you a letter
But why asks the bat as he flaps his wings
I know she cheated on me amongst many other things
Well does that really matter? Asked the crow
You love her still, isn't that so?
And finally the crow said to the bat
A sparrow is a sparrow. It's as simple as that

The Crow and the Bat
(Pt.2)

The crow and the bat weren't walking
They weren't flying
Neither one of them were talking
All of the sudden the crow started to choke
The little frog laughed and he croaked
The bat did nothing just looked at the crow
He must hate him more than he knows
Then the crow suddenly stopped and looked at the bat
And said 'you didn't even help me, what's up with that?'
The bat just looked at the crow and said,
'You're right you know'
He said, 'I hate you more than you know'
The crow asked why and began to cry
The bat said, 'you took the sparrow from me,
Don't you see? I need her back desperately'
The crow gave a crooked look
And the bat looked back
The crow said, 'I'm not with the sparrow as a matter of fact
The other day when you saw us together
We were trying to figure out what to get you,
Possibly a love letter'
The bat started to panic and stared at the crow
And said the only thing there was to say, he said,
'Well at least now I know'
The crow started hovering around the bat and said,
'No, now it's all changed as a matter of fact
Now that you showed your heart, like your fur is black,
I'm going to the sparrow and I'm taking her back
You were worried before and now you have good reason
Now, my old friend the bat, I will commit some treason'

The Morning

By: Great Grandpa William Weatherhead

The morning is a bad time
When you first try to rise.
We look into the mirror
And get a big surprise.
Our eye bags they are bigger,
No matter how hard we try.
If we didn t have so much to do,
We d go back to bed and die.
Eye bags don t bother Grandma,
For she is old and gray.

Back in the old hey days,
When young ones got the eye bags,
Tis a hard thing to cope
Some will take a look at this
And take a pill or dope.
Grandpa didn t give a hoot
If he had eye bags or not,
When he got tired behind the stove,
He d bog down on the cot.

We don t get the rest we need,
And watching t.v. at night
The bags will really puff out
Makes a person look a sight.

Tour of This Brain

Let's get real for a minute
Open my brain and let's see in it
I'll give you a tour if you're ready for a scare
I'll strip myself of everything, show you myself bare
There's some blood and some bruises
Damn, this may be useless
I see some black spots and maybe that's mold
Parts are rotten although I'm not that old
I think before we go in we should put on
some gas masks and some gloves
There is a lot of pity and bitterness in there
but I'm sure we can find some love
There's nothing that's happy or nothing that's bright
I'm thinking someone shoulda brought a flashlight
Let's just go down the stairs and try and find something positive
Somewhere that a smile lives
You follow me; I know this place all too well
This isn't too bad although I know it looks like hell
Now ladies and gentleman if you look to your right
You'll see memories of that night
It was the first night he left for deployment
Now maybe you get part of my torment
Now on your left you'll see a memory of him and me,
It's something you can't miss
Yes that was the night in Hawaii when we shared our first kiss
From that day forward we had our obstacles
Now folks if you'll shut the fuck up look straight
ahead you'll see a pile of skulls
Don't be frightened those are just skeletons of me that are dead
It's ok, I was just a little fucked up in the head

The poison from me is gone, those are just the remains
Yet, I'm sure it can't be healthy that they're still in my brain
Oh coming up next, this should be good
I'd block this part out if I could
You see that black orb floating around
That's the one that kicks me to the ground
That black orb is what fucks everything up
Takes away all my happy thoughts and all my good luck
It just floats around and touches all the gleeful memories
That black orb is the thought of him overseas
Every time I'm happy for just one hour
It floats over and touches it and turns everything sour
So are there any questions for me today?
What's that sir? What did you say?
No, that question's dumb, you go away
Does anyone have a REAL question?
And no, I will not talk to you about him
Why you ask?
Because its, just to painful
Didn't you see all those skulls?
I keep trying to block it out
That's what this tour is all about
He's everywhere he's in my soul and my head
Constantly thinking is he alive or is he dead?
He's in my heart and in my brain
That's why this is driving me insane
He is you in the front, yes you right there
And he's you in the back with the ugly hair
He's the guy in the middle holding the pretty girls' hand
He's the old lady with the walker that can barely stand
He's me and you and the sun and the moon
This tour is over.
My love, just fucking come home soon.

Turnaround Scare

The vamps teeth were sharp tonight
While all the children were a fright
But his eyes were fixed on another victim
Ready to lick her, ready to get some
One with long dark hair
And a back that was bare
And through her bedroom window
He could see her undress slow

Still she didn't notice anything eerie
On this Halloween night
So she turned up the heat and out the lights
The vamp with his thirst readily eager
Was about to pierce her throat like a dagger
In one quick flash he was standing behind her
Ready to kill her
In the darkness
A blur

But she turned around calmly
And instead of screaming with fright like he might have planned
She tilted her head and howled at the moon instead
When her body changed from goddess to lichen
There was no mistaken, he was frightened

He fled the scene in one flash of the light
That's always been her favorite part of Halloween night...

Under The Monster

My tongue feels heavy
Weighed down by these words
The things I speak
Are often absurd
I think I'll cut it out
And throw it away
I'll maybe bleed through the mouth
For a couple of days
Blood will spill
It might make me dizzy
But I'll do some other things
That will keep me busy
Like swirling my eyeballs around
To face the inside of my head
So I can see those disgusting things
And not this life instead
I'll forget all the horrors
Of this outside world
And stare for eternity
At the mind of a fucked up girl
And while my tongue is still bleeding
I'll rip off my arms
Because sometimes I think,
All they do is harm
So, if we recap
Let's see, by now:
My tongue is removed, my arms are amputated
And my eyeballs are inside out
But shit now we have a problem
The smell of blood is getting to me

I'll have to get rid of this nose
So cover your eyes kids, this you may not want to see
Since I have no arms I'd have to break it on the sink
Anything to get rid of this smell
I'd rather have a broken nose
Than walk around, carrying the scent of hell
So blindly I find my way into the bathroom
And find the faucet
Then I wind up and feel the connection
It hurts, so maybe I should sit
The smell of blood is gone
But now I'm fucking hideous
When he comes home,
He's not gunna want someone so ridiculous
So I stumble to my safe
And press the big red button that says "Reverse"
But somehow, I have a feeling
This'll make it worse
Now my eyes are in my arm sockets
And my arms are in my eyes
And my tongue still weighs a thousand pounds
Because of all the lies
I've been trying so hard
To be someone else
That somewhere along the way
I permanently lost myself
I will greet him with stitched up eyes and no arms
And he might not like my crooked nose, or anything he sees
But I think he'll know that somewhere under the monster
Somewhere, there's the real me...

Untitled

Contrary to what others believe
I know you're right for me
I still think we should be together
Even through the harshest weather
What does it matter what they say
Who are they anyway?
I know what my heart wants
And it wants you
Despite what you say now
I know you love me too
~~~
Laughter in the stillness
Chills in the darkness
And I know you're there
A hand on my shoulder
A cold night a little less colder
And I know you still care
~~~
Folgers and Camels
Faded pictures and dull pencils
A letter in a box that you wrote me
An envelope in a drawer with an old key
All of these things are useless, who knew?
All of these things are just like you
~~~
Craziness took control

In a rough spot
I won't always love
What I can't have
And what I haven't got
Are you right for me?
I guess we'll see
It seems like this darkness
Will last for eternity

~~~

How did we go from black to white?
How did we get from day to night?
How did I love you now you hate?
How did we start out so early and now it's too late?

Yes, I m talking About YOU!

Give me a fuckin break
You re nothing

You think I care?
I don t I swear

I say shit to your face
You say it to my back

You suck
I laugh

Gimme gimme that
Gimme gimme this
Smack Smack Smack
Kiss Kiss Kiss

Annoying annoyance
That s what you are
Now go have another drink
Since you re dyin to get to the bar

Drink up boozey...
That s what you do best
If being drunk is a class

You ve passed the test

Rum Rocks
Whiskey Sour
Short Bud
Nope, make it taller

Dirty Tini
3 Olives not 4
Is there any liquor in there
Op...you better order some more

Keep drinkin ...drunk
Keep drownin ...sunk
Keep lying...laid
Keep scheming...paid

Oh you re so cool
Just kidding...fuckin fool.

You think I care about you?
I really don t
Think I ever will...
Nope I won t

Self-proclaimed do-gooder?
Liar.
Liar.

Your ugly pants just caught fire

Double standard, hypocritical fraud?
Yup
If you re a sinner...can you still believe in God?

Tell me again...why do you think you matter?
You talk but all I hear is chatter chatter chatter

Oh calm down...I m not talking about you...

You re over-reacting...really.
Read it again...

I m talkin bout me. . .

Zombies

From tombs to hills
To valleys below
The skies turn black
And the creatures say hello
They break free from hell
And silently escape
Slowly taking over those asleep
And those wide awake
Their arms outstretched
Come for you and me
To suck us into
Misery
Pale faces
And nails like knives
Come for your children
Your husbands and wives
Torn clothes
Ragged and rotten
Bitter and beaten
From being forgotten
They walk steady pace
And never get nervous
And get hungrier and thirstier
As they come for us
Eyes bulged out
Cheeks sunken in
Let the feeding frenzy
Howl and begin
They get off on the shrieks
Of boy and girls

And eating you alive
Is their biggest thrill
Person after person
Meal after meal
Allows them to suffer less
And begin to feel
They stalk the happy
And leave the poor
They suck out the saints
And go to find more
They gather all the sinners
And herd them like cattle
And tell them darkly
To join their battle
The sinners cave in
Like it's the only choice
While the saints die alone
Fighting for their voice
When the city is taken over
And the demons are done
I might have died
Yet, I still have won

Past

"Once I got out of that toxic relationship I was like 'Wow, what an idiot for ever staying', I didn't realize just how bad it was until it was behind me." -CCV

A Hard Past

I focus on how much I love you
But how about how much you love me
You waited two years
You waited so patiently

You lived with a thorn
She constantly bickered and battered you
She left you broken
You weren't used to being with someone so soft spoken

I cried when you confessed just how miserable you were
A whole five years wasted and depressed because of her

You took your time with me
And now I can see why
She was cold and empty
But now I see love in your eyes

I guess sometimes I don't realize just how hard you had it
Putting up with her abuse
Taking all of her shit

I try to be good to you
Treat you with respect and dignity
I try to make sure
You never have to stop loving me

An Unsure Feeling

Living in fear and doubt
That those words will spill from your mouth
And this everlasting terror
Will turning into a very real nightmare

Heart racing every time
That glaze fills your eyes
Don't know if my heart can take this
And break like this
Every time

I want to just believe in the love that is there
But the unsure feeling is everywhere
I just want love to be enough with out
hearing the words from you
God, just tell me what to do . . .

Battle Dust

By: Great Grandpa William Weatherhead

Man and wife they battle,
You'd think it was a must.
Whey don't they shake each other's hand
And leave the battle to us.

The courts are jammed today
With all the battle dust.
Its costs us all a penny
Your money it won't rust.

The salary of the judges,
And the cost of county court
It makes the good tax payer,
Stand right up and snort.

'Tis tough on all the young ones,
When parents go to court,
And leave the little children
Without a home of any sort.

Lawyers they are happy,
They make a real good haul
The taxpayers suffer,
The little children and us all.

Black Rose

Why did you give me a black rose?
The smell of it stung my nose
It had the most horrifying smell
Did this rose come from hell?

Its petals all wrinkled and dying
Do you enjoy seeing me crying?

Why couldn't you just give me a rose
that was red, pink, or white?
Why give me a rose as black as night?

When I asked you this, you looked at
me like I was losing my mind
Do you hate me and did you really
give me this black rose?
Or am I just colorblind?

Bother My Soul

I hate so many qualities that you have
Or is it that I admire them?
I love the way when you have an
opinion you always state it
Or was it that I actually hate it?

You're so confusing
Yet I find it amusing
That you bother my soul
Yet I love you so

I hate it so bad when you're right about things
Or was it that I love the security it brings?
I love the way you tell me I look
good in whatever I wear
Or was it that it annoys me
Because there are so many lies there?

You're so confusing
Yet I find it amusing
That you bother my soul
Yet I love you so

Contemplating

Contemplating what I should do
Am I still in love with you?
Questioning how you make me feel
Is this pain much too real?

Two years I have felt like this
I wonder how much I have missed
Will it ever go away?
Will you ever, ever change?

Not sure, I could live without you
Why would I want to?
Because you give me such disrespect?
I haven't shown you any yet

It's been too long to be this insecure
I don't know how much more I can endure
I should trust you, but can I?
Why can't you answer when I ask you why?

You treat me as less than an equal
Day after day, sequel after sequel
I give up everything just for you
What else do you want me to do?

Corner of the Room

I build it up in the corner of the room
Hoping soon
I can let it out

I pile it up in a corner of my heart
Separating it apart
Waiting to shout

But it's this that I can not deny
I love you
I will not lie

I tell you that over and over
Holding your hand
Crying on your shoulder

But I hide the things I need to say
Repressing them
Depressing me
Day after day

Why did you love her?
Why are you friends with him?
Why don't you tell me how happy you've been?

Maybe someday
Sometime soon
I can take all of this out of my room

Could I Forget?

You left me
Although I really don't think it's fair
You took more, than what was even there

Drop you off, pick you up
Don't call at all, call on time
Make sense of this, reason of that
Do or do not rhyme

Bliss when it's perfect
Hell when it's not
I've forgiven all you've done
But I haven't forgot

Do you love me more than anything?
Or just a little, or just a bit?
I'll forgive you all you've done
But how could I forget?

Crystallized Thoughts

Crystallizing the words I want to say to you
Making them so small and minuscule

You make them feel like they mean nothing
You make me feel idiotic for sharing emotions
So raw and real
Minimizing and mocking everything I feel

I wish just once I could open up to you
Tell you everything you mean to me
But I don't want you to reciprocate with pity

Physically,
I find you more appealing than anything I've ever seen
You turn me on more than you realize,
And that, I really mean

You're more hilarious and adorable than anyone I know
You make me smile from the inside out everyday,
Even if it doesn't show

You pull at my heart every time you leave
You say you'll never hurt me but that's hard to believe

Crystal bits and pieces
They are the small fractures of what is left
Of my feelings, thoughts, and emotions for you

I blend them up so finely that I'll never use them again
But it's hard not to wonder if you let me,
What could've been?

Different

Thunder just outside these walls
Lighting follows its calls
I touch your back
You don't move
You don't whisper back that you love me too

I stare at the ceiling
I burn holes in your back
You only breathe louder
The ceiling begins to crack

Just because you're done with this conversation
Doesn't mean it's over and done with
I start to cry so you can her me
As I wonder what this is

What does it mean that we have nothing in common?
Nothing to share
I wish just a little bit . . .
I wish you would care . . .

Disappointed

I have a sickness
I'm eating myself whole
I hate myself
More than you know

My own judge
And my own jury
I feed off the pain
I feed off the fury

Blaming myself
For what you did
I stood with you,
When I should have hid

It'll happen
If you just let it
I'll tell you what
I sure as hell regret it

Letting walls down
After building them up
Did I just bleed myself out,
to let you drink from my cup?

I filled my veins with steel
So you couldn't get in
And when I let them run red
The betrayal would begin

So easy to hurt someone
So hard to do right
Let's be lazy and unlawful
Instead of putting up a fight

I hate you now
So I'll blame myself
And sit and wish,
I were someone else

I'll take a spoon
And eat away
Wishing I never met you
Wishing you'd go away

I will not cry
As I regret knowing you
And all the shit
You put me through

I'll dissect myself
From the outside in
And make sure,
You never win

I placed you up high
On the most beautiful pedestal
It was so wrong what you did
How could you not know?

So I'll rebuild that wall
And block you on the other side
And feel regret,
That I even tried

You weren't worth the efforts
You weren't worth the tears
You've confirmed all my nightmares
You've confirmed all my fears

Brick by brick, I build
Keeping you at bay

So fucking disappointed,
You turned out this way
Do Something

Touch me just once, is all I ask
On the wrist or the small of my back

And I'll feel better

Say a kind word or two
Gently whisper 'I love you'

You could even write it in a letter

Look at me, the way you used to do
And bite your lip in that way
Say I look beautiful today

Say I'm a good mother or a good friend
Hug me on my way to the bathroom
Even if it's pretend

I'll appreciate it more than you know
If you can just show the feelings I want you to show

Flesh on Thy Own

Burning with passion or rage
Hot blood flowing under skin
Boiling through steaming veins
Spilling out unto bones
Heart beating thirty times to fast
Even visible through a warm breast
As a hammer through a wall
And the Maker so still
Reserved, calm, and peaceful
Does this Maker not see?
It's flesh on thy own
Oh, it would be Utopia!
The Maker's lips turning towards the sky
How gay and sweet it would make oneself feel

Ghost

The ghost of who you used to be
Maybe?
The person I never knew you were
Or maybe I just wasn't sure . . .

Just a former lifetime
I've used up all my lifelines
No one to consult, no one to ask
Forced to looking forward
No more looking back

The ghost of who I used to be
Maybe?
The person I never knew I was
So this is what love does . . .

Help Me!

I used to think about what was done wrong to me
But I've realized that's not fair suddenly

A fallen soul, incorrigible and hopeless
A poet without words, speechless, noteless

I swear to the heavens I love you
So why do I need him too?
I'm lonely·damn! That's no excuse
I'm unchangeable what's the use?

If I promise to stop and never tell you
Will you still love me?
Because that's the only thing that will really help me

I Think For Awhile

I did something wrong but it's not what you'd think
Last night I went out, had fun, and now I can't sleep
I met someone, had a few laughs
Now that it's over, I can't take it back

I had a lot of fun, met a guy, sparks flew
I think for a while, I wasn't even thinking of you
He made a pass but I dropped the ball
He crashed and burned and hit the wall

He was great, so was this other guy a while back too
I think for a while I wasn't even thinking of you
These guys had everything, even more, it's true
But they did one thing wrong, they weren't like you

They had everything I used to desire
Everything that lit my fire
Everything I've ever prayed to have, they had it too
But when I had to make my choice
I smiled and thought about how much I really love
YOU!

I Won

Again, I fall to my knees
Weak as the day I met you
I try to be strong, stand up, and start new
Funny how you knew just what to do

Dirt stains my legs and palms
Blood runs rapid through these veins for you
The grey sky speaks wonders about this heart
And your deception
There is little chance for redemption

The soul can only take so much
And it's been beaten and battered by yours
I'm opening up my mind and closing my doors
Once and for all I'm saying I'm done
I think this time
I have won

July

A perfect heart breaks in July
I'm tempted to ask you why
I have flashes, of memories, of you
Confusion stirs and I don't know what to do
He loves me too selflessly
And all I can do is wish you back to me
It's hard when the weather is warm without you here
Never seeing you again
Is my biggest fear

*

Coffee and cigarettes
It's hard to forget
All the bad times and a shit load of regrets
Tuesday evening and I cry of the memory of you
Thursday morning, there's nothing better to do
A flawless July day
Blue skies with no gray
I set you on the highest pedestal
Could you even see the ground below?
He wants me more than you did
And more than you do
Today is the day I quit...
Quit you

More Than They Do

It seems strangers even see
I'm beautiful
Do you love me?

The whole world could tell me I'm perfect
It doesn't matter because I only want you to see it

My mother
My sister
My best friend
My father

The bank teller
The stranger
The handsome man behind the counter

They will love me
But will you?
I want you to find me
More perfect than they do

Paralyzed

A knife through my heart when I heard the news
I choked when I had to congratulate you
Why didn't you tell me you were seeing someone?
I don't know if I believe you when you say it just begun
I tried, but I couldn't get to sleep
I guess that's just what you do to me...

Paralyzed when you're not around
...So I lay down...

I stare at the ceiling and think of you
Wishing I hadn't heard the news
Paralyzed until morning
I still can't figure out why you didn't give me a fair warning

You still call me up like it's no big deal
I can't stand that this is real
I've been spending my life secretly loving you
Do you secretly love me too?
I tried, but I couldn't get to sleep
I guess that's just what you do to me...

Paralyzed when you're not around
...So I lay down...

I stare at the ceiling and think of you
Wishing I hadn't heard the news
Paralyzed until morning
I really needed more of a warning

Paralyzed
By the thought of you
Do you love me too?
Paralyzed
Until the morning
Wondering why you didn't warn me...

The Way They Used To Be

Why doesn't he laugh like he did
from 1,000 miles away?
And why does do all the things he never thought we ok?

Why do his friends bring up the
painful past and all its hurt?
And why doesn't he look the same
in his faded yellow shirt?

When he gets mad, I used to think he was sweet
But now why does he yell and swear?
And why when I'm sad did he used to console me,
When now he doesn't care?

Why does he abandon me when I
would never do that to him?
And why does he live in a moment of
the past and not the one we're in?

Some things just aren't the same as the first time
Some things just rust and lose their shine
Sometimes we go blind and can not see
That some things never stay the way they used to be

Why doesn't he laugh like he did
from a 1,000 miles away?
And why does he say all the things
I never thought he'd say?

Thorn

A thorn is sticking out of your chest
It's a prickle at best
Its making you bleed right through your clothes
It's all over your face, coming out of your nose

Where did this thorn come from?
Why is it there?
Is it making you weary?
Are you at all scared?

Who gave this thorn to you?
Did it come from a rose?
Who would be so cruel?
Was it someone you loved?
And were you close?

I'm wondering if I can take it out now
Or if it has to stay
Is it the thorn that makes you this way?

I have a feeling many tried to remove it
Many flowers before
But I have something different
I can offer more

Lilies and lilacs and carnations too
All of them were infatuated
None of them loved you

I'll be your palm tree
I don't come with thorns
I won't bruise or break you
I won't make you sore

So if you will accept
If you take my offer
I can love you endlessly
I can love you more than her

I'm taking the thorn out now
I'm sick of seeing you bleed
I know that's what I want
And I know it's what you need
What Would You Miss?

Calls from you and I stay empty
Because you're just way too far away
You call me to say yet again
You're going to be late
I guess you must've forgot about our date

Yet again, you leave without I love you
Your kisses are good
But sometimes words are better
What happened to the days you mustered up
the romanticism to write me a love letter?

Anyway, I'll go now and leave you with this
If you can't change, and I left,
Is there anything you would miss?

Why?

Why don't you tell me that I'm beautiful?
Am I not worth your praise?
Why don't you tell me you want to be with me forever?
Is this just a phase?

Why do you never say I love you?
If you do, why did I say it first?
Do I satisfy you in every way?
Do I fill your hunger?
Do I quench your thirst?

Do you love every part of me?
Why don't you tell me?
Does it really hurt you to say it, that badly?

Am I not funny enough to earn your laugh?
If you say we can do something, why do you take it back?
Am I not good enough to discuss the future with?
Why do you always tell me the truth followed by a myth?

Do I not deserve you to say nice things to me?
Why can't you just say I'm beautiful, even pretty?
Is our relationship really this shipwrecked?
If not, why can't you just tell me I'm perfect?

Nature

"I wanna go on a 'quest' for something. How
do you go on a 'quest', anyway?" -CCV

A City or a Town

I would never pick concrete over gravel
The days and nights combine in the city,
but here they slowly unravel
Nights are actually dark
No city lights to flood the park
Waving at everyone who passes by
People don't give me a weird look if I smile and say hi

Here I breathe in and get a little healthier
No one worries about how to get wealthier
I can actually see the stars out here
In the city, they just disappear

The city reminds me of horns, and yelling, and loud alarms
Someone is always doing harm
This town reminds me of laughter, love, and long walks
You smile just because someone talks

A Naked Tree

There is no greater beauty than that of a shedding tree
But why they choose to be naked
At the coldest time of the year is beyond me
I try to stay true to myself
Not give in to anyone else
But sometimes it seems
As though I'm chasing an invisible dream

Sometimes I feel a tree
Is a lot like me
Standing alone with no armor in the winter
Nothing to give but a twig or a splinter

But the leaves are back, year after year
No matter what they will perceiver
Maybe in its shedding stage, it's just a cleaning
Getting rid of all the unjust beauty in the fall
So maybe a naked tree is the strongest of them all

Carry Me Swiftly

Carry me swiftly through the fields of corn and wheat
Wipe away the beads of sweat from my
forehead from the overwhelming heat
Swat away the bugs and the ticks from my face
Please get there quickly, although this isn't a race

Carry me swiftly through the plains and open the land
When I start to cry, please take my hand
Watch out for the fox and bears
I need you to love me when no one else cares

Carry me swiftly over the gravel and dirt
I'm bleeding and breathing too heavily for this not to hurt
I think you've done you're job, helped
me through my darkest nights
You stood me up when I was too weak to fight

How can I repay you?
Just tell me what to do
Next time, I'll carry you...

Crisp

Buffalo right there on the countryside
The open roads seem a mile wide
The sun setting or rising
Both exceptionally mesmerizing

Open car windows
Hearing nothing but the breeze
Seeing the cows graze with ease

Feeling every emotion- but in a good way
Shifting gears from night to day

Fresh air – gravel grounds
Open sky – soothing sounds

Unexpected detours in all the right places
Friendly smiles on all the right faces

Some describe this as a boring, an untaken risk
I say it's fresh, exciting, and crisp!

Detroit

I remember our drives
Like it was just yesterday they were among us
Getting in our van and revving up that fiery engine
Loud and soothing
Then we'd hit the gas and sail across the hot pavement
Gliding right along and talking
It was as though we'd had a lifetime of stories under our skin
But it had only been a few years
Three at most

We putted along 8 mile and looked at the sadness
The run down houses screaming for help
The businesses in agony
Crying out for a dollar
Or some attention

We'd get a little nervous and then turn back up
Trekking across Gratiot like it was our railway
Hand in hand
Heart in heart
Speaking breathlessly about memories of the future
Thinking out loud about challenges of the past

We'd hit Hall Road
As soon as we'd catch a whiff of outdoor grilling

We'd stop by a fast food joint
Barely satisfying what it is we wanted
We'd keep rolling
Rolling along
Up to Marysville and Port Huron
Lake on one side, the factories on the other

Dusk would creep slowly out of the water
Painting everything in sight a beautiful salmon and light purple
Butterflies would wake up in my stomach
I thought it was a result of the beauty of the pink sky
But it was your hand on my neck
Gently squeezing my muscles
Reminding me for the fortieth time that day
Why I love you

Our journey almost ending and we'd coast along Jefferson Ave
Pull into the park
Our park
The one with the beach and the benches
The one we had a Chinese picnic at
That you turned into a food fight
We'd sit and stare out at the butter
sinking into the endless pond
And I smiled after our kiss
When a yellow butterfly landed on my nose
Reminding me for the forty-first time that day
Why I love you

Finding A Place to Grow

I lay in the meadow
I run in the field
I laugh in the creek

Playing ring-around-the-rosy
Tag
And hide-and-go-seek

Falling fast in love with you
Feeling like a child
When everything is new

Finding things out with you I thought I'd never know
Living with you in the wild and finding a place to grow

Flowers, Trees, and Weeds

These flowers sit in the vase
I'm just going to give them their space
I'll try and not crowd them too much
But everything's too loud to the touch

Silence makes me blind
And being deaf leaves me numb
Sometimes I think maybe
We all just need some

These trees stand in the forest
Their leaves rustling, singing songs of a chorus
I try not to crowd them too much
But everything's too loud to the touch

This pain makes me stronger
And being weak makes me proud
And although that doesn't make any sense
In it, truth is found

These weeds wrap around natures beauty
I understand now that, that is their duty
They try not to crowd me too much
But all of this hurts too much

I lay down in this coffin willingly
This death I died has left me dead
I exit my body, I release my soul
And I crawl right out of my head

Golden Star

From the edge of the eastern boarder
Of North Dakota
To the highest tip of Michigan
The Upper Peninsula
I've seen many things
The beauty astonishing
The nature captivating
The journey
Priceless

Fargo fades out behind me
Not much to look at in the rearview
I pass quickly through Moorhead
And glide along Highway 10
Higher up into Minnesota

I pass small towns littering the highway
Weave in and out of the slow motion pace of these mini worlds
The sun slowly falls into place
Streaking the northern Minnesotan sky
Purples and pinks and oranges

Sunsets always awaken the flutters in my stomach
Tickling my belly with excitement and love

As I climb further north
Inching towards darkness
My eyes may become a little heavy

Stop in Brainerd for a coffee
And to fill up some gas
Fuel for me

Fuel for the vehicle

Switching music tones I perk up
I let the darkness become my beat
I bounce in my seat and scream out the lyrics
Rock –n- Roll
Rock –n- Roll

Duluth comes before I know it
The factories come and pass
Leaving the smog of the city behind, I slip
Tipping south for a few miles
Traveling straight into Wisconsin

Here, the trees become thicker
I lose my peppiness a bit
I focus through the fog
Squint my eyes in concentration

The white clouds low to the ground
Tease my eyes
Make me see things that aren't there
They seep out of the woods
Narrow roads
Thick brush and nature close in around me

Turns and bends every half mile
My knuckles a little whiter
My heart a little faster
My breath a little heavier

Absentmindedly
I turn down the radio
Alone with my thoughts I lace towards my destination

My body becomes shaky

A little numbness oozes into my skin and bones
Subtle trembles through my arms and legs
Lethargy tells me my body needs rest
But I won't stop

I blink my eyes
Hard
They're dry and stung by lassitude
But I hum the tenderness away

Finally, I roll into Michigan
I sit back in my seat
I let out a sigh
Somehow
With the state line
The mist lifts

Everything becomes a little clearer
As I pass through Ironwood
Leaving the miasma behind

Turning up the music I smile a little
Letting the company of the notes and words
Bleed through my soul
Encouraging me

And then
Somewhere around Ishpeming
Something glorious astounds me
Something magnificent

It's breathtaking and holy
It's the sunrise

The first split second I realize
The first moment I FEEL it upon me

My heart warms up
My eyes tear up and drown the dryness
The aches and the pains ebb
As a light baby blue starts to erase the black sky

I see the grey of the pavement
I see the brown of the bark
The green of the trees

When all is colorful again
When all the birds are done singing their morning songs
I see it
The sun
The yellow butter rises from the ashes
Speaking to me
Singing that I'm almost there

And then
Just as the golden star emerges all the way in front of me
I see it
It says:
HAPPINESS: 20 MILES

I soar on to Interstate 75
I exit almost just as quickly as I get on
Sault Ste. Marie
Michigan
*
Him again

Gypsy

Are you a gypsy?
I'm a gypsy
I travel
From city to city

I meet beings of every shape and size
I sit in cafes and draw their eyes

In Atlanta I met a girl
Maybe she was sixteen
She was the most beautifully, saddest girl
I'd ever seen

In Detroit I saw a man
He looked haunted
And I asked to shake his hand

There was a place in Kentucky I met some miserable folks
These people were ignorant and loud
I didn't much care for that town

In Missouri the population was pleasing
I had ate at a bar and shared a beer
And talked to a table of alcoholics about a cure

In Minneapolis I saw a circus
I sort of thought to join them
But to be perfectly honest, I was too scared of the clown men

In Fargo I knew of too many people
So I tried to stay away
But maybe I'll go back there some day...

I Swallowed the Sun

I as I sit here on this hill and think of what could've been
I swallow the sun and think of him
It warms me, but only for a little
I think of a few things that make me giggle
I talk to the deer and the antelope
And swing from the trees on natures rope
In my bikini that's made of leaves and berries
I sit down for tea with the goblins and fairies
We talk about things that only magicians know
And I take time to swallow the sun whole
I cry with the wolves and their wholesome calls
And I bathe with the mermaids in the waterfalls
I cook my dinner with the boars and the sharks
And then fly up to bed with the fireflies and monarchs
I have the monkeys tell me a bedtime story
Then let the mermen and sirens sing to me
It's chilly up here in the trees being the only one
I sure am glad I swallowed the sun...

In The Sky

When the stars in the sky
Told me that you're the one
I cried then I smiled
Then I waited for the sun

When the sun in the sky
Told me that you're coming soon
I cried then I smiled
Then I waited for the moon

When the moon in the sky
Told me that you're it
I cried then I smiled
Then waited for the planets

When the planets in the sky
Told me that this world is ours
I cried then I smiled
And I thanked the glowing stars

In The Spring and The Fall, I Wondered...

On a gravel road the car makes a sound
that I think maybe shouldn't be.
But I kept driving and singing,
and singing and driving.
I wondered, if I were a singer, would I sing louder?
Would I roll down the windows a little further,
for the cows and the horses to hear?
Would they enjoy it, and smile at me?

I came across that old bridge,
the one my old friend would drive too fast across.
I would hit him in the arm and he'd laugh.
I did not think it was funny; my legs were
numb but my heart, full of joy.
But I saw this bridge and I wondered?
If I were a photographer, would I get out and snap away?
Would I sit here longer to enjoy it, to capture it?
To keep it?
To frame it and sell it to a stranger?

I drove up to the hill called Columbus,
as the leaves were on fire with reds and oranges and golds.
The colors flowing together like a crayola box had exploded.
And I wondered?
If I were a painter, would I open my trunk?
Would I get out my easel, and canvas, and brush?
Would I splash the page with watercolors, knowing,
I would never quite capture the true beauty of this day?

I had a picnic in a "No Trespassing" land,
and I was serenaded by the birds.
They sang to me so sweetly, I didn't know the words,
but I hummed along and I wondered.
If I were a guitarist, would I grab it from the backseat?
Would I open the case and play?
Would I strum along melodically with the
blue-jays and humming birds?
Would they ask me to come back sometime?

I drove home and I wrote this in my head,
on an open gravel road.
I did this, because it's the only thing I know.

Missouri

I have a map of Tennessee
On my passenger side seat
I don't really look at it
But it's nice to know it's there for me

Passing through Kentucky
Looking at all of the sights
I feel so lucky
It's only me tonight

I've seen a few other states so far
On this road trip
Just me and my car

But so far on this trip cross country
Nothing quite compares to Missouri

Naked Water Lily

I sit naked on the row boat
I hum a melodic tune
I swim in the sun
And bathe in the moon

I'm stripped of everything
Left smooth, porcelain, & unflawed
With my mind, I entertain the ducks
And wait for their applause

Long hair shiny and straight
Flowing down my bare back
My eyes are heavy and so is my heart
As I start slipping through the cracks

I can feel this is my subconscious
Maybe a little mind over matter
However, I will enjoy my peaceful water
Before the dream, is all but shattered

I am quite comfortable, my skin and I
As I start to row along
I feel amazing being naked and free
In my little, mystic pond

I grab a water lily
And I stroke it with my hands
Then let it slip away,
Like a million grains of sand. . .

Nature

I dream dreams of peaceful things
Things of pleasure, things serene
I sit and watch the stars so still
I perch myself upon this hill
I reach for the moon and sun up high
I sit, I watch, I wonder why
I lay in the meadow and watch miracles pass
I wonder how long this life will last
I lay upon this snowcapped mountain
And swim with doves in natures fountains
I sleep on the clouds up in the air
And dream my dreams with out a care
I cry with the wolves in the forests and trees
I run with the deer and sting with the bees
I fall with the water from the cliff to the stream
And I shine with the rainbows as they gleam
I roll with the waves in the great open sea
I swing with the monkeys in the canopies
I herd with the cattle in the hot endless plains
I ride with the wild boars in their dangerous terrains
I sparkle with the stars and glisten with the sun
I am nature and we are one
I am the jungle I am the sea
I am nature
And nature is me

North Dakota

Rocks and hills
Plains and dirt
Deer and fox
Stained shirts
*

Gravel and snow
Skinned knees
Dust and corn
Willow trees
*

Mud and rain
Open roads
Wheat and grain
Frogs and toads

Road Overload

Me, this motor vehicle, and the road
Here at night with my mind on overload
No one but me alone on this highway
Somehow, in all the commotion I lost the day
The diamonds guide my way
A map of intuitions is what they lay
The moon is hiding; doesn't want to help
Or maybe 'tis busy with someone else
Maybe it's you, taking its time
Hoping and praying it can read your mind
Where are you as I drive alone?
Working? Driving? Sitting at home?
It's peaceful out here on the open road
Here at night with my mind on overload
Leaves blow across the road as I glide into town
I turn my eyes up. My thoughts down.
Now the streetlights help me see
And guide my way as I find my key
Just then, the moon comes out
"Not so fast. I have something to say.
Take your key and come this way."
Then the leaves started to blow a path for me
"Well now," the moon started to say
"I have a wish that I must grant.
And without you here; I simply can't.
So take that key and insert it
In the very first thing you see."
So I started to walk and the leaves started to part
And I was instantly standing face to face with your heart
"So you see," said the moon
"I am never hiding. He just needed help desperately.
Stars do a great job.
But some things should just be left up to me."

Sunny Florida

A place so carefree – it stings me
Back home is where I should be
There the seasons change and are real
Harsh and harder to deal

There at home I am isolated
Aggravated
For the reality of it all
Winter Spring Fall
With out you – nothing means anything

So if I just stay here maybe
My life would be carefree
A picture perfect life I would live in
Be fake and nothing would ever begin

The Freeway

By: Great Grandpa William Weatherhead

When driving on the freeway
Doing eighty-three
Makes you wish you were a bird,
Instead of little me.

Some birds can do eighty
Or maybe eighty-nine,
And chances are they can leave
All the cars behind.

When driving on a freeway,
Your chances are in doubt
'Cause cars are here and cars are there,
And everywhere about.

I'd rather be a little fish
In a lake or brook,
And think of all the fun they have,
Dodging all the hooks.

If driving on a freeway
And you lose a good front wheel,
How do you keep from hitting,
Another automobile.

I'd rather be a good old horse,
On a township trail,
And move along slow and easy,
Just like a snail.

Your chances for survival
Are very, very slim
When driving on a freeway
Be you Ted, Mike, or Jim.

Give me back those good old days,
When there wasn't so much talk;
When Father put on his good old coat,
And went for a walk!

The Leaves They Come and Go

By: Great Grandpa William Weatherhead

I think I'll take to the hills,
And stay for a spell.
All this work in this life,
Can go where you cannot tell.

I love the trees in the late fall
When they turn to gold and red.
And how they play in the night,
When a man has gone to bed.

The leaves play in the meadow,
In the fall with the Old North Wind.
The leaves bounce here and there,
Catch fire now and then.

I like to watch them whirl and play,
For they are gold-read and sleek.
They remind of children in the fall,
Playing Hid and Seek.

Leaves are here a short time,
From spring 'til the late fall.
Man is here a short time,
'Til he gets God's own call.

So people take it easy,
Play like leaves in the fall.
For life seems a short one
For you, me and all.

The Meadow Thoughts

In the meadow, where grasses grow
I lie there sleeping, dreaming of snow
The sun is heavy on my soul
What my mind has to offer, no one will ever know

The long grain washes over, back and forth
I sit and wonder which way is north
Snowflakes of you, fall in my head
With nothing but memories that are now dead

A butterfly brushes against my skin
I realize I may never finish if I don't begin
Something in the air made me think you were there
When I realized you weren't; I got so scared

The wind started whispering secretly
And told me that you are here with me

The Vines

The vines twist and tangle my heart
My body is being dried out like a work of art
Because when the sun is missing
How do you live?
When you never receive
How can you give?
The Earth is cracking, pulling apart
The vines twist and tangle my heart
Here in the open field with nothing but the breeze
When the sun is missing, how can I not freeze?
Even if it's in a desert, where the sand pulls my skin apart
The vines still feel the need to twist and tangle my heart
The ice breaks and drowns me
With the sun missing, how can this be?
How does the warmth pull it apart?
The vines continue to twist and tangle my heart!

Waves

And we build them up
So quickly
So fun

With so much life
We create them
Laughing
Trying

And then they fall
They crash and crumble
Leaving piles
Misshapen lumps on the ground

So unrecognizable
No one even knows what they once were
We build up these emotions
So quickly
Like sand castles

Then they crumble and crash
Just as fast
As the waves rush in
To wash them away

The Game

"You're nothing but a game to me, the only reason
I came here to see you, is to finish it." -CCV

"In the game of poker, I can put the players'
souls in my pocket"- Beausourire

A Broadway Production... starring Evil

Do you like me? If you don't, you will
I'll work my ass off until it's your heart I fill
I'll make you cry and confess you love me
That no one else in the world is above me

And when you kiss me, I'll force myself to blush
Then I'll tell you, you make my blood rush
Then I'll make you hurt my feelings
And make me feel bad
You'll say 'I'm sorry' over and over
Until I'm no longer sad

I'll leave you little love notes and write you special poems
Spend all day with you
And tell you 'I never want to go home'
We'll play board games and I'll even let you, let me win
I'll kiss you gently, stroke your hand, and whisper
What a perfect day it has been

Then the time comes and you tell me
That you want to spend forever with me
Then you realize that I'm not talking back
And I turn to you in my final act
And with a tear running down your check
I'll tell you how great this has been
And smile as I tell you I like you; but I'll always love him

Beauty Kills

In her beauty death is found
She makes them crumble to the ground
Her eyes pierce their hearts
And her voice rips them apart

Her strength suffocates their souls
Her weakness?
No one knows
They say her hair smells like vanilla and sugar
And they fight to the death just to be near her

Outside she's hard, beauty, and strength
They say she's an angel, amazing, and great
Inside she cries and yearns for his return
Looking at all these fools who don't stand a chance
And watching them burn

Being myself only

One by one the roles I played
Slowly begin to fade
Not remembering quite how they were
Trying to remember
Memory astir
You killed them
Made them disappear
Now it's only I that is here
Sometimes I feel lonely
Being myself only
No one else to talk to
No one else to get me through
I must deal with things now as they come
Add them up. Total the sum.
It's not that I miss them, it's really not that
You just love me for me. Why is that?
1 personality 2,3,4,5 too
Without them what will I do?
I used to be scared of losing them
Now I'll just be who I truly am
With you, I don't have to pretend
Putting the rest of me to an end
I died four times now left with one
This is what I was born with. I guess it's better than none.
You finally killed all those girls I once was
I guess that's what true love, truly does

Fool

Precious boy, you made me cry, you took me for a fool
But dear soon you'll know, you're nothing but my tool

You played for me on your guitar
Kissed each other, in your car

Where did all of this weakness come from?
Who the hell have I become?

I didn't intend on being this way
It just happened one day

Strumming along, and writing for me
You're blind to things you need to see

You think you'll hurt me, and that you are in control
But my precious boy, there are so many
things, you do not know

I have committed this crime many
times, just ask the ones before
I'll finish you and you'll finally see,
then I'll head off to do more

My memory won't leave you; I'll burn images into your soul
We've been together only a couple times,
but you're under my control

You can say no, and try to fight it, but it will happen anyway
Don't be sad, my precious boy, I'll be back someday…

I didn't know you had it in you
To be so mean and so cruel
Congratulations:

….

You are still the biggest fool.

Found trust

And I felt bad for the girls who loved you
And I felt bad for the guys I did the same thing to
And I felt bad for how bad we fooled them
You hurt the girls, I hurt the men

You took their innocence I took their pride
I wonder how long all each of them cried
I wonder what they're doing now
If they got over us; how?

How long did it take them to realize we were fake?
How upset were they? What did they say?
What are they thinking of? Are they in love?
Do they still want to get together? Or do they know better?

Through all the people we played
Look at the relationship we've made
I feel bad for them, but look at us
Through all of this, we finally...
                                    Found Trust!

Honest, Kind, & True

By: Great Grandpa William Weatherhead

You ruined my life, you ugly man
You're not the kind for me.
Bought me roses and goodies
And took me to all-night sprees.
You won my love when I was young
What a fool you turned out to be
Why I feel in love with you
Is more than I can see.

Me and my kids live in a shack
And this he calls our home.
While all the time, day and night
Me and the kids, sit home alone.
Whey do men turn sour
Right after they are wed
Does our pretty face and figure
Do damage to their head?

Lord, give me the power to be a wife,
That is honest, kind, and true.
And hope and pray the day won't come
That I'll play the part like you.

if

If I could break something to change it all
I'd shatter all I own against the wall

If stealing would make you forgive me
I'd wipe out all the stores completely

If swearing would help turn back time
I'd curse out the world and make it rhyme

If there was something I could do to take
back the pain I've caused you
I'd do it a million times until you could
finally say, "I love you too"

Just A Few Things about You

I'll take some notes on how to break your heart
But first, I have to play the part
So these are just some things I've remembered
I've been practicing since September

You're a waiter in a restaurant in town
You chuckle a lot and never frown
Your eyes are blue your skin is light
You dressed like a pirate on Halloween night

You have no love for personal space
You have a faded scar high on your face
I know your left ear is pierced
And I've found that your fight is fierce

I like your hands they are smooth and slender
When you work, I watch them in complete splendor
You act as if you're not into your appearance
But you spend too much time on your hair
and clothes not to feel their expense

I've also taken notes on your likes and dislikes
You hate running, like rollerblading
And you and your dad used to hike
You like reading books on fantasy
And at night dream of going there
You like watching movies and making witty comments
And you feel a bit too comfortable in your underwear

You say you used to be a little overweight
Even though now you're thinner

And in high school, you were an all-state swimmer
You love animals but act like with some you get annoyed
You like singing and find music hard to avoid
You act so laid back and I'm sure you mostly are
But honey, that act will only get you so far

You love your parents and you brothers too
You ignore me when I say 'I like you'
You hold your religion close and stick by it
You hate any drama that crosses your
friends and try to defy it

You get jealous easily even though you say you don't
I know you'll cry when I leave you, so don't say you won't
Last but not least I know that you like me
Little doest it surprise me, nor little does it strike me

I'll take my time on you
You'll take a bit longer than the others did
For all your feelings are fairly well hid
You'll fall for me and I'll pass the test as I always do
And give myself an A+ for never sincerely falling for you

Left/Right

A thousand miles to my left
A thousand miles to my right
Which way will I dream tonight?
Normalcy says left
Dreamers say right
I hate struggling with myself in this fight
My head says left
My hearts says right
But what will I do if left is right?
I miss left
But I love right
I just need someone in sight
It's sunny to my left
Foggy to my right
I just want to know how the weather will be tonight

Living with a Criminal

Call it a sixth sense but I can sense
When a man is losing his strength
I take it, run, and keep it for myself
Building up my power and my health

I give him all of his dreams
Make sure he's happy by any means
Be whom he wants before he asks
Only I know I have those masks

I feel like a character in a comic strip
A special cartoon villain with a cool name
Not doing it for fame
Just doing it to watch their shame

Living life on the edge and dangerously
But it's not you, it's me
Wide eyes and caffeine stained shirts
Staying up this long used to hurt
Is betrayal and insomnia a crime?
If it is, it's about time
I should really tell you the truth:
You're living with a criminal who will
steal your innocence and youth

But I'll come home tonight in my special comic car to you
Hang up my mask and my cape too
I love being a criminal, but in one of my prey today
I realized something that blew me away
I felt guilt for once and I know I love you
So I said goodbye to him; I knew I had to
I'm so sick of this job I've managed for so many years
I'm sick of all their pain and even their tears
I'm so sick of all this shit
So today, I left my victims and I fucking quit

Naïve

I bet you smiled on the other line as you lied to me
Laughing quietly because I'm so naïve

You did this to me, so are you proud?
Did you smile as I frowned?
Did you get off when you turned me on?
Do you love making me think you're right,
when you know you're wrong?

I bet you smiled on the other line as you lied to me
Laughing quietly because I'm so naïve

Why lie and make me feel small?
Do you think I matter at all?
You love acting and playing the game
Do you even know my name?

I'm smiling on my side of the line as I lie to you
You're so naïve
Who knew?

Smiling on the other side of the line as you lie to me
Laughing quietly because you're so naïve

Our Curse

On yellow paper, you wrote those words
And in my head they're forever heard
Wondering if you meant them at all
If you did, why don't you call?

I realize now you didn't even know who I was
I guess that's what lying does
I cover it up so very well
You'll never know my personal hell

I resent you for being so cruel
Then remember I am the fool
I lie better than you
You don't even know what I can do

Looking back on pictures of the you I hate
You have no idea that I can relate
Funny how you used to be bad but now I'm worse
This is my, this is your,
This is our curse…

Secrets and Lies

Your bag of secrets and lies
I can see your deception through your eyes
I know it's in the back of the closet
And you know I know it's there
There are little things that remind me
of the old you; everywhere

Why do you keep it?
What does that do?
It's not who you are
It's just the old you
Full of pictures and tapes and letters
Of all of those girls, do I know you better?
Beer and sex
Secrets and lies
How long until the old you dies?

I could throw it away and not a word would be spoken
But then some trust would most definitely be broken
You could move it some place else
And admit he's still apart of yourself
Deep down I know that you're not him
Only maybe a small part of you, where the light is dim
I won't bother you anymore
Just as long as you know, it bothers me
I hate that little bag of secret and lies
Why the hell can't you see…?

Your dirty bag of secrets and lies
I can see your deception through in your eyes
I know it's in the back of the closet
And you know I know it's there
There are little things that remind me
of the old you; everywhere

Smack!

They talk behind everyone's back
Smack smack smackety smack smack
Heather: "Is she?...Oh my God I know"
Carmen: "I tried to tell her, 'I told you so'"
Heather: "Did you her about him too"
Carmen: "Oh my God, I'm like, dude, she's using you"
Heather: "I know right, did you know he is..?"
Carmen: "Oh yeah I know, that baby's not even his!"
Heather: "O. M. G. really, like for real?"
Carmen: "Oh yeah, and what a pussy, did
you hear his favorite color is teal?"
Heather: "You've GOT to be kidding me, that's just sad"
Carmen: "Oh I know, like, that color is JUST A FAD"
Heather: "Oh and like I saw her the
other day and she was crying"
Carmen: "Seriously about what?! It's not like she's dying"
Heather: "Oh right?! I totally know"
Carmen: "Ugh that girl is such a hoe"
Heather: "Oh my God, girl you're so funny"
Carmen: "Oh gee thank you honey"
Heather: "Like seriously you are my BEST friend"
Carmen: "Don't make me cry bitch, besties til the end!"
Heather: "Ok BFF I gotta go"
Carmen: "Ok text me later, hoe"

Now walks up Katie as Heather walks away
Trust me this shit happens everyday...

Katie: "Fuck my life, was that just Heather?"
Carmen: "Ugh, I know her boyfriend
could do SO much better"
Katie: "Oh yeah right you're like her BFF"
Carmen: "Oh ew have you heard her annoying
voice? I wish I were fucking deaf"
Katie: "Oh my God you're so funny"
Carmen: "Oh gee, thank you honey"
Katie: "Like seriously you are my BEST friend"
Carmen: "Don't make me cry bitch, besties til the end!"

The Doctor Of Frankenstein

He makes you a monster
Like the doctor of Frankenstein
You're as much his as you are mine

He talked too much and I knew of a different you
I found out way more than I wanted to
He told of stories of your horrific past
How wide was my gasp?

If I could hurt him as much as I wanted to
I would no longer be with you
Just to slap his face and hear the crack
Just to tell him to go to hell, and not take it back

He made you a monster
Like Frankenstein
When you're with him you're not even mine

You could give me a son, your heart, a ring
But with him in your life, something's missing
If I blamed you as much as I blame him
If I hated you for all you did…

I hate him with the purest passion
I have horrible thoughts that can never take action
I know you take full responsibility
But with out him would it even have been a possibility?

My blood boils every time I hear his name
The sight of him drives me insane
A chill down my spine every time he calls
Praying you won't fall under his spell
I want to trust you but with him, who can tell?

He made you a monster
Like the creator of Frankenstein
Every time you're with him,
I hate that you're mine

The Game

And I thirst for more
Hunger for another taste
Cruel by nature
Letting nothing go to waste

Using men
Abusing them
I tried so hard to stop
Controlling men
Enrolling them
I just couldn't stop

Something about them wanting me
Made it so hard to quit
But he was still there still haunting me
So I continued this shit

Turns out, he was the same way
Hurting the opposite sex
Neither of us knew what to say:
This was our everlasting hex

We turned our backs on that game
And we're starting a life together
We are finally done living in shame
And we'll be together forever

the Pill

By: Great Grandpa William Weatherhead

You had your day, you painted doll
With high heels and mink coat.
You stole, you lied, you cheated me
Ran whiskey down your throat.

You smoked like a steam engine
Till your mink smelled worse than a barn;
You can leave me now and don't return
Or I'll maybe do some harm.

The Pill made a fool of you
It has ruined your life for good.
With your beauty of early years
You could have been what a mother should.

I'll miss you much when you are gone
Thinking of the early years.
What a fool I was to go for you
It brings a man to tears.

I'll try again some other time
When you are over the hill.
And hope that the next time around
There'll be no such thing as the Pill.

Who the Hell Are You?

I keep finding little secrets everywhere I turn
In the quiet, dark corners of your life
I look at them and burn
Choking on questions and too many tears
Each new one I find, confirms all my fears
Did you change completely, 100 percent?
Did you really say what you meant?
Or are you a liar, a cheat, and a thief?
And am I just young, dumb, and naïve?
I hate who you were; I despise every part of it
So do I hate you now? Is the old you who I get?
I'd like to believe people could change
And that you did too
But how can you erase something,
That was such a huge part of you?
I find these clues and I start to shake
It's too much to swallow, too much to take
If I were an outsider looking in
I would say, "Only an idiot would stay with him"
So will I leave? Or will I stay?
Do I really want to spend the rest
of my life living this way?
I could leave and there are a million
other things I could do
But the problem is, I'll always love you
My heart is much bigger than my head
Even though I know where all the signs pointed,
I know where they led
Living in constant fear that you'll leave me
That's the worst feeling; believe me
A few last questions I wanted to ask
Are there things in your life you'd like to take back?

Did you change?
Who are you now?
Are you a better person somehow?
Do you love me?
Whole-heartedly?
Would you listen if I played?
Would you cry if I left?
Or smile if I stayed?
Or am I something you'll regret?
Would you spend your life with me?
Will you stay for eternity?
And if I vanished tomorrow,
Would you go back to doing what you used to do?
Or have you truly changed?
Just who the hell are you?

Why Do People Do It?

By: Great Grandpa William Weatherhead

When a young man gets married,
His head is in a whirl
For he does not know a chipmunk
From a little old gray squirrel.

He dresses in his Sunday best,
He is really in a stew,
He has so much on his mind,
He doesn't know what to do.

His new wife is a nice one,
Full of pep and glee.
She wears high heels and tight pants,
Quite a "chick" is she.

Both go to work six days per week,
The cash it really flows in.
Then all of the sudden something snaps,
And the living is real thin.

The payments pile up for this and that
'Tis more than they can bear,
About that time they both wish
To vanish in thin air.

If a man had a brain in his head,
He'd stay single and he'd roam;
And when he went to bed at night;
He'd really sleep alone.

It's tough for the young men of today
Who tries to make a home.
When he dreams of the day gone by
When he slept alone.

So brace yourself like a good man should
And make those payments alone,
And dream of the good old days gone by
When we all slept alone.

Drinking & Sex

"I never once understood their addiction, then you came and it changed my perception.
Ending these words you always knew, the one addiction I've known is you." -CCV

Bitter

Its bitter as it goes down
And I start to drown. . .

Sitting here staring at this empty room
Hoping and praying to see you soon
Nothing makes the second hand go faster
It still feels like last year. . .

Its bitter as it goes down
And I start to drown. . .

Silence cuts through my body
Shot one, two. . . twenty-three
Nothing to touch my skin but plastic and metal and cotton
I feel hollowed out but somehow still rotten. . .

Its bitter as it goes down
And I start to drown. . .

Laying on this pillow, acting like I actually sleep anymore
Staring out this window, acting like you're actually going to come through the door
Putting on a facade that you'll call
My illusions mean nothing at all. . .

Its bitter as it goes down
And I start to drown. . .

Talking aloud like you can actually hear
Maybe if you were near
Spraying myself with perfume, that no one will even smell
This. Is. My. Hell.

Nothing but TIME can bring you back to me
. . . Honestly . . .
Its bitter . . . put the bottle down
before you drown

Blocked State of Mind

The way your hands find my body in the morning
The way you set me off with no warning
The way your lips find mine in the dark with no trouble
The way you touch the small of my back so soft and subtle
The words are impossible to find
You just have me in a blocked state of mind
The way you touch me, sends my body on fire
The way you kiss every inch of me gives me a burning desire
Everything about you I admire
Every time I'm with you I get higher and higher
The way you make me feel is an unexplainable kind
You just have me in a blocked state of mind

Corner Saloon

By: Great Grandpa William Weatherhead

I walked into a corner bar
To meet a man I knew.
The air was thick with filth and grime
Kind words were very few.

They stand up by the bar at night
If they sit, they can not rise.
Most of the stories that are told
Are often ball-faced lies.

Why are men in these joints?
Do they hate their homes?
Chances are the wife and kids
Are sitting home alone.

They cough and sneeze from filthy air
And this filth, they bring back home.
If they had the brains of a yellow dog
They would not leave the family alone.

'Tis not safe for women and children
To stay alone at night
While men are in the Corner bar

Mugging all bar maids in sight.

That's why good women sometimes go bad
'Cause they sit at home at night
When he comes in at one a.m.
She is ready for a fight.

He comes in late at night
He's roaring like a lion
Says "old lady" don't forget
This old house is mine.

She gets up in her nightgown
You can't kid me, you Goon
Pack up your junk, you drunken slob
Go back to the Corner Saloon.

Drinking Alone With Ghosts of You

I stay up until my eyes bleed
Wanting what I can't need
Drinking all alone with ghosts of you
Nothing much else to do
I click the T.V. off there's nothing on I wanna see
Unless it's you here next to me
I pour another glass of whatever this is
And down the color, the smell, the fizz
I search for something to listen to
But I don't want to hear anything unless it's you
So I turn the radio off and my memories up
And walk to the kitchen to pour another cup
Remember that time you fell down the stairs?
I laughed so damn hard although I was really scared
Or the time we drove from Fargo to Detroit in one straight shot
We made it time to ring in the New Year but barely beat the clock
This couch is sure lonely at 3 a.m.
Thinking of would could've been
What would we be doing now if you were here?
I push it away and go get another beer
On the way to the fridge more memories sneak in
Like Gavin DeGraw, remember when we went to go see him?
Or Oreo Pie, man we could eat that stuff couldn't we?
I remember everything so clearly
Fuck it, I'm gunna grab two beers not one
Maybe that'll get the job done
Get you outta my head so at least I can sleep
I should get some rest considering I can't even eat
Insomnia? Yeah, maybe I'm an Insomniac
I will be until I have you back
Well, looks like this loser is outta booze
With you missing from my life I'll continue to lose...

Drinking Is a Sport

I see the people surround me
Vision closing in and getting blurry
I try and act like this is fun
But its not, its fucking dumb
Oh yeah, lets dances our faces off
And when you turn down a shot of tequila
have someone call you "soft"
Shit, I wish I never started drinking
I feel like I'm sinking...
So what?
It makes me a little happier for a minute?
I drink a drink with out knowing what's in it
So guess what? I LOVE self inducing headaches
And puking my guts out until the toilet breaks
I guess it's cool to take shots you know will make you sick
That you realize it the morning will make
you feel like a shit ton of bricks
I OWE it to myself though to get dumb and act stupid
Did I really just fall on my ass....YUP! I did!
Pretty amazing to chug a beer until you spit it out
I guess that's what being cool is all about
And the money....yeah that's another thing
Shit, how much cash should I bring?
Ah hell, how about fifty that should be plenty
Nope, not even close...not quite, not really
Because my dumb ass decided to by a round for the bar

Fuck, I think I have another twenty out in my car
Don't you just love feeling outta control?
Like liquor just straight up took your soul?
I'm kidding. I hope you didn't answer yes
But we deserve this right, after all our stress?
We DESERVE to not be able to walk straight
And make ALL KINDS of dumb ass mistakes
After all it's been SUCH a long week
This is my high point...look at this awesome peak!
Shit man, I think I look COOL right now with my hair in knots
Make up streaked face because of those shots
This is pure class man, stumbling to bathroom
Just thinking in your head "fuck I gotta leave soon"
But NOPE, don't worry I'll stay out until three
And have more shots that will almost kill me
Ah shucks, drinking is so rad
Getting accused of being too drunk and
responding "I SWEAR I'm not that bad!"
That's always fun when some drunkard tells you YOU'RE too drunk
I just wanna scream "SHUT THE FUCK UP!"
Yup, alcohol is just so much fun
Fuck I wish it didn't make me feel so numb
I LOVE waking up broke and ill
Gimme a glass of water and 3 or 4 pills
Look at how many relationships and friendships it wrecks
Just one of the great perks and amazing side effects!
Hey kids! Drinking makes you act super cool and not stupid at all
Nope, I lied...but you fell for it didn't you...you just took the fall
So if you like acting stupid, making yourself sick,
and doing things you wouldn't normally do
Drinking is DEFINATELY the sport FOR YOU!

Drinks, What Else?

I went out and it was fucking disgusting
The shit tasted like water rusting
The first sip was bad the second was worse
This poison is alcohol, wrapped in a curse
And I ordered another and I don't know why
By the second sip of the second beer I wanted to die
My tab's gunna be heavy and my heart even heavier
But I ordered another martini and asked for it dirtier
Then I said, damn I feel like a Mary Bloody
"Uh ma'am do you mean a Blood Mary?"
And I said "who the FUCK do you think
you are?! DIRTY HARRY?!"
I said 'I said what I meant and I meant what I said
Now make me a Mary Bloody before I kick you in the head'
And after that Professor I'd like a Old Fashioned please
I think that's what they call it.....aaaahh, geez
I guess I don't really know WHAT I want
Seems like I've been saying that a lot...
I'm sitting here with a fucking liquor store in front of me
Seems strangers can even see
They must be able to tell I'm nuts
So I raise my glass to them and buy 'em some shots
Fuck it why not, it's not like I'm broke
I may have some money but I'm still a joke
No matter how many Manhattans and how many beers
I'll never get rid of my deepest fears

Oh but you don't know me very well
I'll sit here alone in my personal hell
And try to drown out every last thought
The booze killing my memory is the last chance I got
I've tried everything else, I tried to be good
And I'd lay off the drinking if I could
But it numbs it, if only for a little while
While I sit here with you all and put on a fake smile...
And I hope you all know I'm not who you see
Only he knows the real me.

Drunk

Laying alone, dark, and waiting
Feeling scared without you I'm suffocating
Because you're the only place, I want to be
But you only call when you're mood is enhanced chemically

Can you ever call me when you're sober?
Or is that just too much to ask?
You've been drunk since last October
How much longer is this going to last?

You said the most romantic thing when you called
Then I realized you were drunk
Now I don't know if it's sweet at all
Or if this is just my luck

Lying alone and waiting
Without you I'm fading
Can you call me when you're sober?
I pray it's sooner than next October

Dumb to Feel Numb

It's so dumb
Take a sip of wine, to feel numb

It's so stupid
Take a drink of whiskey, thinking it'll help you like cupid

It's so idiotic
Pouring a glass of beer, just to get sick

It's so pointless
Taking a shot, to act like a mess

It's so silly
Drinking & driving, I mean, really?

It's so sad
Boozing, getting so drunk, you get mad

It's so wrong
Liquor up, just so you can sing that song

It's so depressing
Pass out, to avoid the problems you should be addressing

Drinking? I don't know, I do it, I just don't get it
It's hard to love doing something, when you know you regret it

I Wanna Start Again

Little needles poke into my skin and I cannot breathe
I just want to let you in, let you, become me...

My heart gets so tired from beating so fast
Once my energy lets go, I want it to last
Your breath is so heavy and my vision is blurry
My blood gets hot and the air gets colder
My pleasure multiplies, as the night grows older

And I have to think — of how to breathe again
And I have to blink — to realize this is real life I'm in
And I have to know — that it is not a sin
And once we're done — I wanna start again

We build to a climax
Your lips on my skin makes my body tremble
My muscles shake and then relax
This night here, no other could resemble

And I have to think — of how to breathe again
And I have to blink — to realize this is real life I'm in
And I have to know — that it is not a sin
And once we're done — I wanna start again

Finally, after so damn long
We're reaching the ending and making it strong
I never knew how close we could be
And all at once; you become me

Liquor & Longevity

By: Great Grandpa William Weatherhead

The horse and mule live 30 years
And know nothing of wines and beers

The goat and sheep at 20 die
And never taste of Scotch or Rye

The cow drinks water by the ton
And at age 18 is almost done

The dog at 15 cashes in
Without the aid of rum or gin

The cat in milk and water soaks
And then in 12 short years, it croaks

The modest, sober, bone dry hen
Lays eggs for nogs, then dies at 10

All animals are strictly dry
They live sinless lives and swiftly die

But sinful, ginful, rum-soaked men
Survive for threescore years and TEN!

And some of, the mighty few,
Keep drinking until we're 92!

Men Will Fall

By: Great Grandpa William Weatherhead

There is a thing that goes on each day
And men they really care.
And men hope that it won't stop
And vanish in thin air.

Men watch it on the streets
And in the city halls.
They really enjoy it very much
At the dance and at the ball.

Men watch it on the beach,
When women are in tights.
They will talk about it all day
And dream of it at night.

Oh, why do women do this
On the beach and at the ball?
That wiggle when they walk
Causes good men to fall.

We really love the wiggle,
All good men say:
"'Tis the best thing that happened
Since the good old Model 'A'."

My Corner Saloon

Calling you from a telephone booth
It keeps ringing so what's the use?
My dress and heels, and my big floppy hat
We're all wondering, where you're at
Are you at the corner saloon with your friends?
Drinking that dark liquor that you think mends?
Is there a pretty lady sitting at the bar?
Wondering if she can talk to you, see just how easy you are?
Will you bet a hundred dollars of our money, in a losing game of pool?
Will you fight the biggest guy in the bar, just because he made you look like a fool?
Will you laugh so loud everyone in the bar laughs?
I wonder if when you get home, you'll try to see where I'm at
Will you care if I packed my things and went away?
Or will you just go up to that Corner Saloon the very next day?

No Friend of Mine

I open up the refrigerator
There it is
It stares at me
I think I saw it wink

Drink me
Forget all of your problems

Drink me
Act outrageous

Drink me
Mask the pain

I open the cupboard
There it sits
Staring back at me
I see it smile once

Pour me
You'll feel much better

Pour me
Drown the sorrow

Pour me
Let me be your friend

Predator vs. Prey

Do you not understand my desire for you?
Do you not want me too?
'Like' isn't enough
It just won't do
I thirst
I hunger
I yearn for you

In your absence
I weep and moan
If I can't have you
I'd rather be alone

I'm starving and my plate is empty
But you're the only meat I see
I'm thirsty, dehydrated, and needing juice
Unless it's from your veins it's just no use

Subtlety is my weakness
Give me two seconds alone with you,
You'll know what I mean
My eyes will tell you things you've never seen

I'd rather go hungry, than feed off anything but you
Like a predator looking for prey
So until I can have you,
I'll starve every day

Replacing You with Booze

Since you've been gone there's something I've been doing
I've been missing you so much so I fill the void with boozing

I miss your touch and how you feel
So I drink a Stoli Water, with a giant orange peel

I miss how your voice sounds so smooth that I melt with it
So I reach high up in the cupboards for the
cheap, dusty bottle of Black Velvet

I miss how your lips taste when they touch mine
The closest thing I've found so far is Raspberry Wine

I miss how you smell, all man, and so comforting
So I down a liter of scotch, the scent is still lingering...

I miss the way you look at me, with pure lust and desire
So I get the hottest thing I can find to make me feel
the heat, I think they call it a Prairie Fire

I replace your love with a little alcohol
I don't think it matters at all

I still feel a hole where you used to be
No matter the amount of vodka, rum, or whiskey

It numbs it a little, but only for a night
I know none of this is acceptable or even close to right

Scotch and champagne and tequila and brandy
None of these things brings you back to me

Not a margarita, daiquiri, pina colada, or bloody mary
Could replace the sweetness, the delirium,
or the buzz that you give me

You're my own personal high, my inebriation, my buzz
You're my soul, my heart, my head, and my love

So I'll put down the bottle, turn away the shot
Before I lose you forever and before I start to rot

Same Ole Same Ole

I go out and I can't breathe through the crowd
I try and think of you in my head but it's just too damn loud
This whole scene is getting old
The same stories told and told
He said, she said
Who slept in who's bed
He did what?
She did who?
Drink number one, now lets shot gun beer number two
Shot 3, 4, and 5
Fuck I don't even feel alive
Stumble to the dance floor although I don't like to dance
Push away the guy who doesn't stand a chance
Get the keys and drive when I shouldn't
Then let the alcohol bring me to bars I normally wouldn't
They check my I.D. and I get way too talkative
Did I just say that, oh shit, I DID!
Find the bathroom with my girlfriend
Lady Gaga? Fuck, I love this song but they're playing it again?!
I need some rock and roll in a hurry and I'll take another beer
Here's to you, here's me, CHEERS!
Let me buy us shot number 6
Then head to the dance floor for this dumb remix
Look at this guy, he thinks he's the shit
Does he know he's not a pimp?
Look at this chick, she's talking smack

I'm drunk and ready to fight, bitch better watch her back
Fuck, the lights are on?
Is it time to go?
Only when I'm bored outta my mind does time go slow
Call me a cab and get one for my friend
I'm gunna go home alone and try to mend
a heart that isn't meant to mend...

So hung over I can't stand, I can't eat
Fuck that alarm is too loud, I shouldn't have had that last drink
I can't think of anything that doesn't make me sick
Can't talk, and walk, can't smell
Sunday Funday you say? Ah....sure, WHAT THE HELL!

Sex

It's beautiful or it's sleazy
It's complicated or easy
It's fucking, and then it's slutty
Or it's making love, but then it's cheesy

It's hard or fast
Or loud or soft
It's in the attic or a parent's bedroom
Maybe the beach or the loft

Girls love it or they hate it
Do guys love it or just like to bait it?
It's messy and it's sensual
And everything but factual
Its fingers and hair and love and lust
It's them and him and you and us

It's him and her
Or him and him
Or her and her
Or us and them

It's gay and straight
And experimental and bi
You're low or tired
Or excited and high

It's black and white
And brown and gray
Its night and summer
And winter and day

Its races and ethnicities
And all times in the day
Its prejudice and judgmental
It's something that won't last but will always stay

It's fun and boring
And unsafe and wrong
It's short and meaningful
Or it's beautiful and long

You're 15 or 40
Or 52
Old to it or practicing
Or very, very new

It's this and that
And that and this
I envy the days
That you could make love with just a kiss

Skirts

By: Great Grandpa William Weatherhead

Why do females go about in skirts
Halfway to their "butts"?
You'd think that cloth was getting scarce
Like lots of other stuff.

They have no pride of any kind,
Some from sixteen to sixty-three.
Even Eve in the garden of Eden
Had sense enough to use leaves of a tree.

What will happen to those precious knees
Chilled by ice and snow.
Aches and pains will get those girls,
Before they really know.

Cover up like girls of old
To meet the cold and snow
And you will feel much better,
Most everywhere you go.

Do not wear those silly skirts,
No matter what the name.
'Tis those two-bit designers,
That put good girls to shame.

Starvation

I am so hungry > starving for you
There is other meat > nothing will do
Lay on my plate > naked and bare
I'll devour you > until nothing's there
I would eat you whole > leaving nothing to waste
Consume you over and over > the sweetest taste
Until I see you > I'll stay forever starved
You'll need no preparing > you're perfectly carved
My mouth is watering > yet my palette is dry

You are doing this > you are my...
Starvation...

The Need

I need to feel full again
Until this emptiness inside me is whole
You don't even know how long it's been
Only he could really know

I've been itching and scratching for months now
And I'm feeling and fighting the need
I don't really know how
Nothing can fix this desire for speed

I need your breath I need your heart
You don't know how long I've been waiting
I need your skin I need every part
I'm sitting here loathing this, sitting here hating

Just come back prepared and come back ready
And I'll make it worth your while
Come back with lots of breath and I'll try to
keep mine from being so heavy
I promise to make you smile

The Wiggle

By: Great Grandpa William Weatherhead

Sit in your car on any street
And watch people walking.
All are going back and forth
Most of 'em are talking.

They talk about the income tax,
And also about the crops,
And listen to the gossip
In the old Barber Shop.

One thing men have not figured
If they did very little.
Why in the world do
Some women wiggle?

I had an idea many a day
Though my lips were always sealed
But if the truth is really know,
'Tis cause by old spike heels.

Women of yore didn't have the wiggle,
And they were surely made alike.
They wore low heels and simple clothes,
But they didn't have the spikes.

White Russians Come and Go

I took my first sip when I was almost 22
What the fuck did I just do?
I held off so long and tried to be good
Dodging the peer pressure, I like I knew I could

It was a White Russian, how it stung my throat
I started to get hot, and took off my coat
It was in a casino, with my mom and him
I drank down the first glass, of what might've been

I stuck with that, for a little while
Until the cream and vodka, killed my smile
I searched for something sweeter, that wouldn't make my smile fade
So I grabbed a four pack, of Mikes Hard Lemonade

Cranberry, Hard Berry, and Lime too
I still asked myself, what the fuck did I do?
Some things so sweet, eventually turn sour
They lose their innocence, and all their power

Finally I tried something, I knew wouldn't let me down
So I ordered a cranberry, with a double shot of Crown
It pierced my poor tongue, but I liked the pain
It skipped the buzz and went straight for the brain

I broke up with Mr. Royal, after some crazy nights
And decided to go with something that would produce less fights
So I took his advice and went with a beer
What do ya know, now it all seems so clear

Not so sick in the AM and easier on the bank
I don't get too rowdy and I don't get so frank
All along, it's been there for me
Just like how I met him, on the shores of Hawaii

But the beer lost its shine, although my man, he did not
Now I'm left searching once again, and he's all that I got
White Russians and Beer, they come and they go
Is there such thing as a perfect drink, the world may never know. . .

I just shoulda stayed as smart as I was at the ripe age of 21
Instead of drinking, and thinking: "What the hell have I done?"

Strength & Life

"Let's just look on the bright side of things,
that's the only side there is." CCV

And I Think

And I think I'm gunna make it if I try
I'll run a little faster
Walk a little straighter
Stand a little taller
And know its okay to cry

I've been trying to get by now for over 3 million years
Though all the battles, wars, and the tears
Coming across an ocean I know I can take
And making decisions that are too hard to make

And I think I'm gunna make it if I try
I'll run a little faster
Walk a little straighter
Stand a little taller
And know its okay to cry

Love is a service I know I can give
I know I can handle it
And he can teach me how to live

And I think I'm gunna make it if I try
I'll run a little faster
Walk a little straighter
Stand a little taller
And know its okay to cry

Be a Good Man

By: Great Grandpa William Weatherhead

Try and be a good man
While you are on this earth
It does not hurt to have some fun
If 'tis clean and a friend it does not hurt.
Treat the wife like she was human.
And she will treat you well.
Go to church with her on Sunday
The "reward" only the Lord can tell,
Treat neighbors fair and square
Always give a helping hand.
And you'll go down in history
As being a real Good Man.
If you go a drinking
Take the wife along.
Even if you stay all night
To the break of dawn.
Try to be a Good Man,
Honest, kind, and true.
And the wife, she will love
Most anything you do…..

Beauty from Pain

Sinking in
To this couch again
Sad and lonely
It begins

Late night sitcom reruns
Burn my eyes
With out him
I'm something I despise

Lazier than I should be
But not quite a bum
He steals all my tears
And then some

I feel my stomach,
It's stirring around
I can hear my tears
Fall to the ground

He leaves my motivation
I'm motivated by a cracked heart
But it can't be broken
When it's not fully ripped apart

Days'll pass torturously
And I'll bleed from my brain
Creating visions and words
That will keep me sane

Do you pick up a pen?
Or a camera?

Or a guitar?
Or do you just pray?
Or hope?
Or wish on a star?

Funny how we're motivated
By the things that cause us pain
Creating beauty and masterpieces,
From things that are insane.

Burdened

I am drowning in the blood you shed
I am deafened by the words you said
I am undeservingly living for the life you led
I am burdened by the cross on your head

I try and not feel guilty, for being a sinner
I don't pray every time, I sit down for dinner
I take your name in vein
And I do some things I shouldn't
But if I could stop right now,
I know I probably wouldn't

I can't wait until the day
I swim and bask in all the blood you shed
The day I hear angels, at the words that you've said
The time when I know you died PROUDLY for me
That day I'll wear with you, that cross of thorns with out misery. . .

I'll fold my hands before each and every meal
I'll feel the things that are so good to feel
I'll use your name only in prayer
And when I die, I'll visit you there. . .

Choices

On my right there's an angel
On the left there's the devil
In the middle there's just me
A strong but lonely rebel

I flick off the one on the left
Then I flick off the right
Only I control day
Only I control night

I hold my head up high
And a walk straight ahead
I'm not scared of the living
Nor am I scared of the dead

We are all born and raised
And then we all die
We all breathe when the sun is low, medium
And when it's high

Everything is relative
Like sinning and learning to forgive
We all do good and evil
For this is the life he wanted us to live

So although there are good choices
And then there are bad
You are the only one who can make them for yourself
So try and look back to be proud of the life you had

Complicating

I feel dead but I can not die
I feel depressed but I can not cry
I hate but I can not kill
I'm sick but I'm not quite ill
I'm in pain but I can not feel
I'm not in a nightmare but this isn't quite real
I curse but I don't swear
I feel sad but I don't care
I'm confused yet I get it
I'm pissed but I won't quit it
Do you understand what I'm saying?
Or is this just plain complicating?

Now I'm dead but I'm still alive
And I cried so I feel revived
I killed and now I don't hate
I'm no longer sick because I finally ate
I can feel and I'm not in pain
And my nightmares are dreams now and gone is the rain
I swear now to you that I never curse
And I feel happy now instead of worse
I don't really get it now but I'm not confused
I never get pissed now because I never get used
Did you just pick up on this and everything I'm saying?
Or was this just too damn complicating….?

Constant Wind and Thunder

The winds blow fiercely
However, I cannot recognize the direction
As in my own life
It's like a reflection

Similar to the thunder rolling
My heart pounds severely
I can hear it constantly
And oh so clearly

Reveling in the glory
That this storm will soon end
I'm hoping and praying this city,
And my head will soon mend

But even in the silence of this settling storm
I sit and hear the wind, I'm sure
For I fear there will never be a day
When there isn't a constant wind and thunder

Excuse of Bleeding

Have no idea where I'm going or where I should be
I don't even have the excuse of bleeding...

Perfection surrounds me
And I cannot breathe
Drowning in greatness
Silently

Not knowing what I'm here for haunts me
Even when I can't use the excuse of bleeding...

Running backwards
Trying to catch up somehow
Failure at bay
But success, my silent vow

I feel helpless, useless, and self-pitying
Even without the excuse of bleeding...

Suffocating on losing
Not knowing how to win
Tired and wishing I was finished
Even before I begin

Waking each morning facing endless torture, wanting, and needing
Wishing I had an excuse for doing nothing...something like bleeding...

I have nothing to show
Except for a lifetime of 'tries'
No excuses or reasons
Just left being a person I despise

Fear paralyzes me
As I choke on self doubt
My blood runs cold and veins freeze with questions
As I try desperately to shout

At least if I were bleeding I could let it out and cry
Instead of being this person, who holds it all inside...

Geek

I've been called chicken legs
I've been laughed at
And tormented
I've had braces
And zits
And embarrassing moments

I cut my hair too short once
I looked like a boy
Didn't help that my nose
Had not yet grown into my face

I dressed how I thought was cool
Turns out
It wasn't

I tried so hard to fit in
Tried to crack jokes
Or laugh at the ones I should

I attempted sleepovers
And boyfriends
And sitting at the cool table
At lunch time

I'd pray for the lunch hour to end
It was too lonely standing next to my locker
For a half an hour each day
While everyone else huddled
By the water fountain
And laughed about things
That I always suspected were about me

I've cried in my room at night
Wishing the school year would be over
I've dreaded riding the school bus each morning
Wishing I was with in walking distance

I've thought about running away
Or quitting school
I've thought about asking my parents to move
I've thought about all the options

But then
It was summer
And I didn't have to deal with it

The New Year began
Filling my heart with fear
But on the first day of school
Something had changed
And I was cool again
No longer a geek

No one stays a geek forever
And even if you do
Embrace it
Because looking back
I've never respected myself more than I did
When I was one

Maybe I'll always be one. . .
Deep down

How I Call

How can we measure wisdom?
It's not by scholastics nor popularity
Rather by experience and integrity

How can we measure strength?
It's neither by weight nor endurance
Rather by hardships and inner independence

How can we measure selflessness?
It's not by how much you are loved
Rather by your relationship with Him or Her or It up above

I call it not a religion
But my relationship with God
A soul who claims to be neither a saint nor a sinner
Is truly a fraud!

I Love My Son

I love my son
My baby boy
I love his tantrums
And his toys
I love his eyes
They look like daddy's
I'm not even sick of sponge bob
And crabby patty's
I love our fights
Ok maybe not
But since Chad is gone
He's all that I got
I love his hair and how it smells
I love his attitude
And the truth he tells
I love how he mispronounces every word
And I love the way when he's messy he looks absurd
He's so cute covered in my make up
Or juice or markers
I love the way he says Co Co and how much he loves her
I love how much he misses his dad
Although it makes me way too sad
I love that he looks like him in every way
And that he asks about him everyday
I love that he makes fun of me like his daddy does
And how he gives me kisses just because
I love our handshake and our bath times too
If you've never met him I feel sorry for you
He's just like his dad in every way
He asks about him everyday. . .

I Must

I see your pain and it's cutting right through me
I see your tears and their tearing me in two
I know what you are feeling
So this is what I must do:
I must fight. I must charge
I must end this pain for you
I must curse. I must kill
I must die, but only for you

I see the way the demons haunt you
And it's affecting me more than you know
I feel the way the burden feels on your back
And I'm crumbling to the floor
I hear the way the angels treat you
I need to help you-I must do more:
I must destroy. I must hurt
I must end this pain for you
I must hunt. I must lie
I must die, but only for you

I know all the terrible deeds you have done
But I have done some too
I recall the moments you broke me
I remember I once broke you
I know that inside your heart is silvers gold
And I know now that I must not give in
I must not fold:
I must help. I must pray
I must guide you through this agony
I must give. I must love
I must need you as much as you need me…

I'll Be Okay

A downward spiral on what should've been a perfect day
But honestly, I'll be okay
You hurt me more than I ever thought I could've been
But that's what makes me strong enough to stand again
My heart was in the palm of your hand
I laid it there for you to hold
You dropped it and bruised it
I've never seen you so cold
A downward spiral on what should've been a perfect day
But honestly, I'll be okay
Funny how you didn't notice you slapped me in the face
It's a feeling I want to, but never could erase
It seems overnight you've changed completely
I guess some things were never meant to be

In A World So "PC"

In the days it paid to be "PC"
I don't think I'd be very happy
I'd wallow around not being myself
Trying to be please everyone else

I'd put on my lipstick a shade or two lighter
And have to be a pushover even though I'm a fighter
I'd sit on my chair and not get up to dance
I'd never play poker because I wouldn't take the chance

They'd say, walk like this and talk like that
And I'd say, I've never been one for friendly chat
I'd have to bite my tongue when I wanted to scream
I'd have to put my life on hold and continue to dream

I wouldn't be very good at being "PC"
I just don't think I'd be happy
I'd dress and talk like someone else
I couldn't stand not being myself

I'd laugh a little bit quieter, and that'd be sad
Because I think the sound of my laugh, makes people glad
I wouldn't cry as hard when I was upset
That's a life, I just don't get

If I think gays are beautiful and everyone's perfect
I couldn't live in a world where I'd be considered a reject
If I think guns are cool and eating animals is great
Who the fuck are you to try to debate?

I think that'd be a waste if I had to hold back who I really am
Because those who really love me, love it, and I love them
I couldn't live in a world that was so "PC"
Because then I couldn't truly be me.

Let Me, For I Am

Let me drown
For I am too weak to try to tread
Let me bleed
For I am too lazy to make a tourniquet
Let me fall
For I am too dizzy to hold myself up

Carry me swiftly to my grave
I have already given in
Bury me in the darkest cave
Bury me with my sins

Let me starve
For I am too useless to hunt for myself
Let me thirst
For I am too dehydrated to go to the well
Let me hold in my tears
For I am too proud to let down my guard

Carry me swiftly to my grave
I have already given in
Bury me in the darkest cave
Bury me with my sins

Lightening Boats

Lightening boats
Carry the women of this world
Does it give men chills?

Thunder roads
Drive the men of this world
Do they drive to the ladies or the girls?

She rides on rainbows to her destination
Calling the boats and cars
Then collects them all sends them off to Venus and Mars

Looking Forward, To The Past

In the light of many things
This bring me no happiness
Only sadness, for the days gone by
Come and gone like the summer
The winter
The spring and fall
Leaving us empty and wanting more
Always looking forward
Or behind us for some sort of justification
Never living in the moment that we worked so hard to get to
Always loving the "waiting" and "anticipating"
More than the gift of the given moment
Then it is gone and we yearn to go back
When in the first place it was never enjoyed as much
As it was meant to be
Slipping into the clothes we've waited to wear
We are so anxious
Laughter now still in the images that are frozen
Looking at photographs of life gone by
We can keep those forever
Look at those, and remember,
Just how much we looked FORWARD to looking back
All we are, all we do
Is look forward,
to the memories. . .

Mask

The part of me I love the most
Is the part that you can't see
The part of me I'm most proud of
Is the part you wouldn't agree

I wear a mask in front of you
But you think it's the real me
I just wonder what you would do
If you knew me differently

You've know me longer than most people have
And it doesn't even show
Because the part of me I love the most
You will never know

You're too locked in your tiny box
To see the world from my point of view
I've tried to show you different angles and sights
But there is just no use

You have your judgments, your preconceptions and your stereotypes
And none of them are even kind of close
To ever being right

What if I took off my mask that you've made me wear for so long?
Would you kick me out of the family?
Or say I didn't belong?

What if I peeled back a part that you thought that you once knew?
What if I was black instead, or Asian, or Mexican or blue?
What if when I pulled this back, I was gay instead of straight?
Would you hate me after all these years,

just because you couldn't relate?

Or what if I was a Republican instead of a Democrat?
Or instead of being Christian I told you I have no religion
What would you think of that?

I'll wear this mask every day, but only around you
Because you're too scared and simple-minded to ever see the truth

My Best Friend

You taught me how to tie my shoe
I'm not sure what I taught you
Played Barbie's until we were way too old
Built snow forts until we were way too cold

Together we learned to drive our cars
We dressed up like our favorite movie stars
You were there for support when a boy broke up with me
And we got to be wild and crazy when we went to Hawaii

Most friends don't get to experience half as much as we do
I can't believe I have a friend like you
Together through boys, dolls, make-up, and
all of our make believe and pretend
You're my laughter, my love, my strength
And you'll always be my best friend

My Sister and I

We stop by the small gas station and fill up
My sister and I
Everyone stops for a second just to say hi

We grab some soda and sunflower seeds
On a Sunday like this, what else does anyone need?
We pull out to familiar back roads
No one else know the secrets each of them holds

We drive silently for a while
My sister and I
Just sit and watch the scenery go by

We finally discuss life and everything in it
And wonder how much better life can really get?
We see all sorts of animals and creatures as we drive
And realize how much fun it is to be alive

We pull in the next small town to get some ice cream
My sister and I
And head for home on our sugar high

We pull into our tiny town with supper ready for us
And go upstairs to wash off the dust
We sit on the porch after our meal watching the sunset
And wonder how much better life can really get?

My Son

No one can make her laugh like he can
Even when she's sad and down
He can make her smile through the frown
He can make her heart skip a beat
She's so glad God gave them a chance to meet

He's the light in her dark room
He's her hope in a world of doom
No one else can compare to him
He's her prayer in a world of sin

He's the best thing that ever happened to her
When she found out about him, she wasn't so sure
But when she saw him, she knew he was the one
Her life changed when God gave her a son

Pegs

Seems to me
That this should be
Something we should never see
If you don't stand up
You won't fall down
Then how will you ever appreciate the ground?
I try to walk
I talk and talk
I open this heart to break the lock
If you don't stand for one thing or maybe two
You'll fall for three and four
And then you'll learn to hate the floor
Easy things are hard to do
And hard things are the best for you
So I gave up completely before I knew
Now I'm standing on these three legs
That seems once were only tiny pegs

Purgatory

I swim in this fire, in this melting pot
Soul evaporating and my stomach in knots
The God's call down and try to lure me out
But not they even know, what this is about
I don't know why but I like it here
Being alone with my pen and my beer
Crying crystal tear drops that no one can see
Being someone, they don't want me to be

I fly in this ocean, and crawl in this dirt
I take this potion, to wash away the hurt
I cry like a lion, and sting like a bear
I attack like a flower, and roar like a hare
Wanting something, not knowing what
Getting nothing, with this door that's shut
So I call back up to the God's
They ask me what the hell is wrong
I say I have no answers, I expected you to know that
They say before you leave, make sure you want to come back

So I settle for the middle, where nothing is good
Nothings big or little, everything's I would, and I should...
It's not that bad but it's not that great
And I start to pray for a brand new slate
Not wanting to go down, but unable to go up
I relish in the memories of His blood in a cup
Wishing I knew more than I know now
I'd pledge my allegiance to Him, make it my solemn vow
So I charge like the tiger, and soar like an eagle
I'll be as loving as a dolphin, and as loyal as the beagle
Fighting the fire for fairness and freedom
Killing the cancer to climb to His Kingdom
I'll say good bye and fuck you to the evil that surrounds me
The love of theses Gods will always astound me

Questions? Questions? Questions?

Do you play chess or poker
Or are they the same?
Can you control them with your mind
Or are they luck and chance games?

Do we all laugh and dance
And do we all cry?
Or do some of us hold hollow hearts
And forever lie?

Is your blood purple or blue
Or is everyone's red?
Will we all be re-created
Or simply rot after being dead?

How long is forever
And does that scare you?
Would you rather go on being yourself
Or start over as someone new?

Do we all love and like
And do we all hate?
Do we pick our paths
Or is there really "fate"?

Does everyone hit things
And does everyone scream?
Or do you let your anger out
In nightmares and dreams?

Are the "butterflies" the same to you
As they are to me?

275

Or do we feel things and see things,
Differently?

Is my red, your black
And is your hat my shoe?
And when I say "old"
Do you think "new"?

Is your sky green
And your sun yellow?
When I say "goodbye"
Do you hear "hello"?

Do we even exist
Are we really even here to find?
Or are we mere thoughts and images
And particles of the mind?

What if all of this a movie
Not real, but A "reel"?
And what would you do, if you wake up as a blade of grass tomorrow,
Unable to feel?

Is any of this clicking for you
Is it making you think?
And what if we all turn to dust,
The very next time we blink....?

Reveal

A drop falls for unfaithfulness
A muscle flexes for braveness
I feel inhumane that I made
A muscle flex, a drop fall, and a heart break
You are strong but I make you weak
My mystical power makes me a freak
I don't want the power over you
There are so many things I could do
Why can't I just be strong and tell you
All the truth I wish you already knew
Instead of pieces, I wish I could do it all at once
Why is it hard when I know what I want to say?
I wish I wish it would go away
Crawl out of my head and into my mouth
Spill from my lips into the air
Swarm your ears without a care
It would be all over if I could just say
Now matter what, I cannot stay

Smiling In His Sleep

My little boy dreams in color
I know this, because I'm his mother
I hear him cooing and softly humming
I know he must be on to something...

I see him roll over, and smirk in his sleep
His face so peaceful in the dim glare of the T.V.
His blanket all the way up to his chin
Not dreaming of where he's going or where he's been

He doesn't have scary nightmares
No dreams about monsters or bears
He doesn't dream about friends or cartoons
Or all of our lazy afternoons

He dreams about playing up in his room
On HIS idea of a perfect afternoon
He's not dreaming of things that make him sad or mad
Because when he's smiling in his sleep, I
know he's dreaming of his dad...

Sticks & Stones

Why doesn't he think before he speaks?
How does he not realize how much his words hurt?
They sting and bruise for weeks
Leaving me numb, subdued, and hardly alert

Sticks and stones may bruise me
But words will scar forever
They last longer than a wound could ever

A bruise goes away within days
But the pain from a terrible word will echo in my body for years
Causing thousands of questions and millions of fears

Sticks and stones may break my bones
But words will always hurt me...

Storm against the Rages

Light is seeping in through the darkness
I will hold on to my faith through the mess
I will not back down from the things I want
Even if it's something I am and you are not

I will swing my fists at all of my haters
And tell them all I'll see them later
I don't have time to listen to them
Hypocrisy is what turns women to girls and turns boys from men

I will not hear the negative words of those who don't know me
Those who act like they love me, but never show me
The static gets louder with all of their words
They speak things of ignorance that are quite absurd

The anchors that bind me to this place
Are nothing compared to love that can not be erased
I have to leave, for I fear I am drowning here
But none of these memories will disappear

I will storm diligently against the rages and the questions
And I will easily ignore all your outrageous suggestions
I am astonished at the arrogance of the simple-minded
It leaves me feeling shocked and blind-sided

If you never leave then you will never know
And if you never know, then you won't ever go
Get up and do something out there, before you judge me
For those of you who know my secrets and scars; I'm glad you love me

It will be a good thing for me, but I will leave you with this
There are so many things that I will sincerely miss...

Streets on Fire with Rage and Grace

It's alive but cold
Places like this, never grow old
The streets are on fire with rage and grace
Maybe I'm just too damn nice for this place

Where the concrete meets trouble
Emotions grow by the double
I'll drive 14 hours to get there
I'll get a new tattoo and maybe shave my hair

I'll speak to strangers about a place to the West
And tell them of the friends that I liked best
I'll let them know that the people in that town
Seldom made me unhappy and seldom made me frown

I'll get my nose re-pierced and buy some more belt buckles
And make sure when I walk to my car, there is white on my knuckles
I'll get a job and make new friends, maybe get a new car
And find comfort in knowing, if I need it, home isn't all too far

I'll find solace in the small dirt roads I find behind the alleys
And put my guard up when I enter the bloody heavy rallies
I'll look back on photographs of sinners and the saints
And laugh at the memory and the picture that it paints

I'll move to the place where life is fast and hard
And keep a trick up my sleeve; it's called the Ace of all cards
I won't forget my p's and q's but will probably curse more often
But remember that the things you all taught
me, will never be forgotten

I'm going to the city where the streets are on fire with rage and grace
But I'll come back often, to visit this place
I'll miss the town with humility, the town
with views different from my own
But I'll never be further to reach, than a button on your phone....

The Box or the Show?

No idea where to go
Do I stay in the box or go to the show?
Hundreds or Billions?
Make a few or possibly millions?
Live with the fish or with the leopards?
Run with the Devils or with the Sheppard's?
Surround myself with music and glam?
Or stay where I get judged for who I am?
Be a needle in the huge, over grown haystack?
Or stay put, in first place, exactly where I'm at?
Noise and hustle and bustle and hurrying up to wait?
Or slow paced, laid back, "who cares if you're late"?
Living where people are open-minded and accepted?
Or staying where liberal ideas are easily rejected?
Back yards with room to run?
Or a nice house with a room for sun?
Knowing everyone and feeling special, like the T.V. show 'Cheers'?
Or going out with a few people here and there for a couple of beers?
Gravel roads and sunflower seeds?
Or living just to live, just because you need?
A place where there is always something to do?
Or somewhere where they'll always love you for you?
I could live here or there or near or far
It really doesn't matter, because home, is where you are...

The Ones Who Fade Away

God I think I'm slipping
Or they're slipping away
I'm scared and frightened
Because it turned out this way

In the end,
all the big and little things
All add up,
to something like a dream

I choke on tears
and try hold them back
As all the photos and memories
start to fade to black

They come and go
like waves upon the shore
Each more meaningful, and beautiful,
than the ones I saw before

I jar up the foam
from the ones who really matter
And try to hold on to them
Before the jar can shatter

The photographer, the singers,
the painter, and the poet
They all mean so much to me,
and they don't even know it

The one who's unusually outgoing
The one who can sling a bottle

The one who plays the guitar
And the one who should be a model

My heart beats uneven,
in sync with certain things
The third of every heartbeat
Is the memory, of a friend, who is now nothing but a dream....

The Place That Washed Away the Pain

In this morning
The storm took away my pain
It washed it long gone
With the wind and the rain

It cleansed my soul
And cleared my heart
Then took my guilt
And tore it apart

This morning in the darkness
I feel completely okay
That my life up until now
Has turned out this way

Staring out the window
At the puddles of rain
Thankful that the storm
Washed away my pain

The leaves that are dancing
Are telling me I chose the right thing
And to just wait and see
What the future brings

I'll move on and away
From the gravel and the dirt
But will always be thankful
The storm washed away my hurt

I'll move to the concrete
And the mass and the noise

285

I'll pack up my favorite things
And my two favorite boys

I'll cry as I drive there
And smile as I cry
But in the bittersweet fog
I'll know that I have to try

When the winds that pass me
Blow across my face, and whisper there will be rain
I'll always be thankful,
For the place that washed away most, if not all, of my pain...

The Young
By: Great Grandpa William Weatherhead

The young have a
A lot to learn,
From childhood, 'til
The time they get old,
They won't believe, or
Nothing they are told.

Father Time will take
Care of this, the young
Can really be sure of that.
They will listen someday
When youth is gone,
And they are old and fat.

So listen, young people
Fair and fine.
Whoop it up all you can.
There is day not
Far away, you'll meet
Old Father Time.

People that have lived
They year, and met
Old Father Time
Know what it is to
Be on a pension, though
The living 'tis real fine.

Young people of today
Don't wish the years away
Away, they'll go fast
Enough you'll find.
'Cause just around the
Corner, so it seems
Is Old Father Time.

Thoughts of Thoughts

Celebrating the rebirth of my soul
The cause of justice was satisfying and whole
A man can go all his life with out knowing
He is the master of his own fate
Its sad most don't realize until it's too late
God gives us life and life is full of choices
Take control and listen to the voices
Live how one wants to live
Do what one wants to do
Execute the right path for yourself
And live for no one else but you
~*~*~*~*~*~

I'm the punk girl who listens to country
I'm dressed in black but you should see my colorful family
I don't smile in front of you
But I laugh behind your back
I read a book a week but when it comes to school I lack
I wear my country boots with my nails painted blue
You criticize me but who the hell are you?
You wear Abercrombie and Nike
And I don't give a fuck if you like me
It's funny how you think I care who you are
Or where you've been
Oh, excuse me, what was your name again?
~*~*~*~*~*~

Called out from the heavens
Was a voice filled with might
I looked up with no one in sight
I thought it was God
And thought I was right
~*~*~*~*~*~

Is it possible to love something you hate?

To bend the rules to fate?
I can't understand why I want you
I don't want to, but I do
You are so bad for me it's good
I won't say no even though I should
You're like the little vile I know I shouldn't take
You're the exception I know I shouldn't make
You're the delicious poison
That goes down so sweetly
You're the delicious poison
That I know soon will kill me
~*~*~*~*~*~

So I reached inside myself and dug around
For the part of me that was rotten
Problem was, it was all of me
There would be nothing left if I cleaned myself out
I would be empty
And I don't know if that's better or worse
Less or more
And I'm going insane
Therefore
I ripped out my frozen heart and my dried out guts
Beside that, everything else was bleeding excessively
And I thought it might last forever…
How long is forever…?
~*~*~*~*~*~

The moon hangs above the Motel 6 sign
Seems like in this place God pauses time
The seconds hang in the air
Minutes hanging in nowhere
Cars rush by a few stories down
People have things to do in this town
Just a passerby
Nearly driving by
But I'll take a break
As the moon hangs above this Motel 6 sign

~*~*~*~*~*~

When feelings of happiness is what I lack
I sit and cry tears of black
Sometimes it takes so long
To shake the feeling that I can't go on
My tears are never clear
Because I always fear, the end is near
Never is my cry soft enough
To only cry a couple of tears
It hasn't been for the past two years
So every time I cry and try to hold back
It's still just enough to turn
My tears a shade of black

~*~*~*~*~*~

Making love until the sun comes up
But you're always thinking nothing
But you're always doing something
Tomorrow I have to leave
So let's just believe
That I can stay here another week
I don't want another winter without you
It's going to be winter number two
The days go fast
But our stares are long
And come tomorrow
I'll be gone...

~*~*~*~*~*~

You look familiar...
Are you by chance Agony?
I seem to pass by your way-
Quite often, it seems
Is there something you want from me?
If there is-just ask and be on your way
Pain & Suffering have already
Asked for far too much today

~*~*~*~*~*~

There is a storm stirring up in the back of my mind
An escape route is so hard to find
They all say they care but end up leaving me
This will be my future as well as my history
Hail in my heart
Hail in my head
Hail in my soul
I pray for sunlight instead...
~*~*~*~*~*~

All the terrible shit you did
All of the truth you hid
All of the lies you made
All that time living in the shade
I know now you are just like me
I hate the way we used to be
I hate all the things we did wrong
But I knew I loved you all along
~*~*~*~*~*~

Tonight I lie and try to sleep
Adding yet another day without you with me
Tonight is night 423
Thoughts of you talk to me
I try to write, play music, and eat
Anything to get my mind off you
But the fact that it's night 423 still haunts me
And your ghost has got me beat
Lighting flashes and for a moment I forget
Just sit in a daze while the sky is lit
Then it's right back to you
And soon this will become
Night 552
~*~*~*~*~*~

Death is a funny word; it's kind of like love
No one knows when it's coming
Or where it's going to happen
It's all a big surprise

You should've been prepared
But it's too late by the time you realize
~*~*~*~*~*~

Tears form from behind blackened shades
Hidden as the perfectness fades
Lips swell and eyes pucker
Knuckles burst and veins crack
Nightmares full of color
Dreams with screams and thunder
Life like this
What if it really is?
~*~*~*~*~*~

Anticipation
A burning sensation
It's down to a week
Compared to a year
Seeing you has never been so near
There's a surrealness in the air
So real it's like nothing's there
Fearful for some reason
Been waiting season after season
You, I, and conversation
A room unfamiliar
~*~*~*~*~*~

Who's that guy over there?
I swear I've seen him somewhere
His eyes so mysterious
Makes me delirious

Tired; Not Weak

When we have to part
My heart
Does not break
But it cracks
So you can take
A piece of it back
With you
Who knew?
How much overtime my heart would do

When we meet again
It's as if we've never been
Apart
And you place that piece right back in my heart
But always know
That when you go
You can take that piece
And we can share a soul

When you're away
Day after day
It's easy to say
So if I may
I'll let you know
That I love you so
So when you're away from me
It's plain to see
That until you come back
And as the hours pass
And with every week
My heart is only tired! Not weak!

Younger Me

Want to put a rock on your head so you don't grow
Tuck you into bed so nothing shows
Act like you're my big sister when I'm sick
Open the last fudgesicle but let you have a lick

Try to get an annoying song in your head
Race down the white snow in our Barbie sleds
Reminisce in the kitchen when the day is done
Talk about the guy of my dreams until the moon is gone and we see the sun

Up in the bathroom I put make-up on you
And even though you don't need it, I tell you what a little eyeliner can do
Teach you how to put gas in your car
Go outside and find out which one is the brightest star

If anyone asks what's important in this life to me
I would say, it's not a house, clothes, or money that makes me happy
It's my little sister
Because not only is she family
She's my friend and simply a younger me

Magic & Myth

"What the hell am I doing talking to a little petal? Well, Jordan talks to Whoppers so it can't be that strange." - CCV

Black Licorice

When we met, it started with a lie
You told me you were a pilot and that you could fly
You told me you weren't in a relationship
And that there were only five girls you ever kissed
You said you would come visit me over Christmas
But Christmas came, and you didn't

You're a liar; an imposter
You're the guy that I'm in love with
You're a jerk and you're a fake
You're the one that I go home with
You leave a bad taste in my mouth
like that candy in a dish
Wow, I just realized you're a lot like black licorice

So you say you were much too drunk
To remember sleeping with her
You say that night you didn't come home is all a blur
Honey, you almost had me going
Almost had me running for my money
But you have to remember
Now matter what you do, you
can't bullshit a bullshitter

You're a liar; an imposter
You're the guy that I'm in love with
You're a jerk and you're a fake
You're the one that I go home with

You leave a bad taste in my mouth
like that candy in a dish
Wow, I just realized you're a lot like black licorice

You're like that horrible itch in my eye
Wow, you're like a bad, ugly, unwanted sty
You have to tell me the truth, just let me know
Is it worth sticking around or should I just go?
I guess since you're not going to answer
I'll just answer myself
I'll just pack my bags and go get someone else

You're the flavor that nobody wants
You're the last item to pick off the shelf
You're the kind of cheap candy
that everybody leaves
For somebody else

You're that disgusting after taste in my mouth
And now I'm just too scared to kiss
Damn, I just figured out
You're my Black Licorice~

Black Magic

I wandered along the ground all snowy
Hoping no one would know me
I held my wand tight in my hand
And trekked across uncharted land

I chanted a chant of old black magic
And tried to forget all my old bad habits
Like licorice whips and lemon drops
And loving you and lollipops

I wandered along this dreary highway
Hoping that they wouldn't find me
I held my potion tight in my hand
And trekked across this mapped out land

I chanted a chant of witches I once knew
I tried so hard to forget about you
So I took a sip of this poison, this potion
Then all the sudden everything was in slow motion

I started to think of you and me
And then so clearly I could finally see
I need you so much I would die for it
Which is why I try so hard to forget

I can't think of you because then I am in pain
I can't remember your face or think your name
Because if I do I fall into this hole
You're the only true love I'll ever know

So I'll wander endlessly until you return
And watch the pages of this horrid novel burn
I'll chant a chant to get you back
And we'll live with the leprechauns and all the black cats

Candy Eyes

I licked a lollipop and it tasted like a tootsie roll
I only sucked on some fun dip but now I'm full
Those pop rocks I had were all over my bed
Now this gut ache has got me wishing myself dead

I ate some smarties and but I don't feel any smarter
Those sweet tarts need to be tarter
Your lips taste like sugar
And your eyes look like root beer bottle caps
I wonder how long this sweet tooth will last

I tried some licorice but I didn't really like it
There's punch to wash this all down but
I'm fairly certain someone spiked it
Andes mints and snow caps too
None of this is as sweet as you

I'd rather have you for one of my snacks
I'll give up this poison once I have you back

CARNiVAL

The carnival and the fair all but shut down
In the darkest part of their happy town
Just getting ready to lure the innocents in
Ready to put on a show, give some rides, and begin

The two-headed woman right off, killed a parent and three boys
And the tallest man in the world, used them as toys
The faceless girl tied up the town's doctor
and took him as her lover
And the ring master charged an outrageous cover

The tight rope walkers sliced and diced all the fat people in town
And the clowns cut smiles into all who frowned
The ticket takers and the games hosts had a deadly battle
And the carnies drank the blood from all their cattle

Three people were beheaded by the man who ran the fun maze
He had to pay back the Juggler with new props one of these days
The fortune teller named Zelda knew all the their futures were ill
For the carnival was in town and ready to kill

From the fields outside of town, all you could hear
Were the muffled screams of the people in fear
You had one way to survive, but it didn't
mean you could leave easily
The carnies said, you can die a fun death or join
us as we move on to the next city…

Cloud Thoughts

There we were in a yesterday
I had a dream of tomorrow and it was today
That the world would be wrapped
in a blanket of clouds
Then my destiny would be found
So in that yesterday
When I dreamt of today
The sun was hiding
Didn't want to play
But the clouds were there
Floating in nowhere
And let me know what would come to be
And I found that forever it will be you and me
~*~*~*~*~*~

Clouds
When clouds of gray
Stray my way
I fight them off
One by one
Until the battle
Has been done

301

Dream?

I sit here listening to the rain drip drop
I kind of wish it would stop
I try so hard just to wake up from this thing
I think they call it a dream
I'm not so sure it is quite a nightmare
But somehow I'm still scared
It's not quite black and white
But I see no color either
I think maybe its sepia or grey
Or maybe it's neither
There's something in it like de ja vu
Or someone I used to be or that I once knew
I'm not sure where it is
I'm getting really sick of this
It's like I'm home but I feel homesick
Maybe this is it
Maybe this is when I'll die
Go up to Heaven
Reach the sky
Is this a dream or is this reality
Oh now I get it...
I finally see...

Empty

A faucet drips
In an empty room
Constant annoyance
Everlasting doom
Loneliness ate me
Swallowed me whole
An empty heart
Took its toll

Sadness full of laughter
Broken dreams shattered
Fell out of a green sky
And Mother Nature cried

A teaspoon of pain
A handful of insane
A candle lit
I'm just a name they'll forget

Fairytale

Life was hard
Love can make a heart break
Into a thousand pieces
Tears freeze on a cold day
And the song of the soul
Always knows
When the heart misses

But to him she looked like Snow White
In Cinderella's gown
He sees Sleeping Beauty in her eyes
As she cries
And he gives her the crown

Her heart like Belle's
But he's not the beast
Because he's like every good price
He makes the pain cease

Fear can be so cruel when you're not ready to be afraid
It's unrelenting and it's callous
So it's served its purpose
That's why it was made

Magic

Inside my head
Grows a peaceful garden
One where you are happy
And full of joy
This image is all I have left
Because I gave it all up
To pause suffering in your life
Your happiness is truly mine
~*~*~*~*~*~

Inside my head
Grows a secret, mystical land
A place where I can see you again and again
Surrounded by all my favorite things
Like you, your eyes, and rainbow rings
~*~*~*~*~*~

Your eyes are like the sun
Blinding but hard to turn away from
Your whole is like the end of the rainbow
My rainbow, my pot of gold
I am your cleanser
Picking up all the scraps of the shattered wall
The one that once bound us
I am your moonlight
Creeping in your room, letting you see

Rainbows into Ashes

Rainbows into ashes
Lightening crashes
Lucky Charms
Sounding off clown alarms
Silver and gold
Dust into mold
Hell to heaven
Heaven to hell
Someone ring the division bell
Meadows in black and white
Zombies at day not night
A wolf and a ghost
Some milk and some toast
These are things I think in my head
When I try and go to fucking bed
Will he live or will he die
And then I really start to cry
Is he in danger as I think?
I try to scream but I can't speak
So I think of tornadoes and rivers
And creepy things that give me shivers
Like demons and people I love who are dead
Get me outta my fucking head
I'm trapped here and I can't escape
Can anyone else even relate?
I don't wanna live in Pandora's Box
I'd rather die with the fish and the fox
Can't reach him because he's overseas
So I'll try and think of bumblebees
Wrap my mind in something warm and wet
Why am I not asleep yet?

Rainbows Rainbows
Ribbons Ribbons
Tell me God, am I forgiven?
I feel screwed up though you say I'm not
But I'm gunna have to disagree: and disagree a lot
Why am I thinking of Batman and Superman
Thinking of how they would kill Peter Pan
Then I think of Cinderella
Then Beauty and the Beast...
Was her name Belle or Bella
I wonder who would win in a fight
I think Snow White would take the night
Sleeping Beauty is too damn lazy
What's wrong with the bitch?
I thought I was crazy
He's sneaking back up again
I miss him so much
I want I need I feel his touch
I'm gunna cry so I fight it away
And think of Thanksgiving on Christmas Day
Or Halloween on New Years Eve
Or atheists having something to believe
Chad, just get out of my head
Unless I know for sure you are not dead
Because this unknown is just too much
I want I need I feel your touch
I can't keep waiting until you call
So I'll think of Alice in Wonderland right when she took that fall
That'd be cool if Spiderman saved her
That would've really caused a stir
Am I still talking?
Shit, I think I am
I just miss you and your eyes
Fuck and Damn.
I feel those tears coming up one more time
So I think what if dollars were dimes

What if stars were cars?
And Venus was Mars
And new meant old
And hot was cold?
And horses were dogs?
And bricks were logs
What if I were the REAL Dr. Seuss
Fuck I'm crazy I think the screws in my head are loose
What if boys were girls?
And boring times were called thrills?
What if clovers were bad luck?
And loose meant stuck?
What if the sun was the moon?
And we all called 6 o'clock...noon?
What kind of world would that be?
Are you following me?
Oh my God, my phone is ringing
I think I hear my heart start singing
All at once I'm normal again
Because the caller I.D. says it's him
"Hi Jordan,"
He says,
"I miss you so much,
I want I need I feel your touch"

The Butterfly and the Whale

The whale and the butterfly held hands
Walking into that foreign land
Knowing they might get judged
For loving who the people didn't
think they should love

The whale had a nice tie on
And the butterfly bought new heels
Knowing they all would whisper and hate
Although they could never know how this feels

The whale said, "well this is just great,
Talking to a bunch of people that can't relate"
The butterfly just hummed and said,
"I have something that might ease your head"

She fluttered up and kissed the whale's nose
And said, "That didn't help, I suppose"
"No, it was perfect, and so are you,
There are just some things, I don't want to do"

She just smiled and then wiped the tears away
And said, "It'll get better, someday."
"Maybe you're right," the whale said.
"Do you have one more kiss to ease my head?"

The butterfly smirked so sweetly, it
gave the whale the butterflies
And she whispered, "I have kisses
for you, that'll last a lifetime"

Weeping Willows

crawl up inside of myself
trying to be someone else
erasing all the memories
like the smell of burnt willow trees
flying on this boat that I just learned to drive
feeling numb and dead, but mostly alive
deleting the distant thoughts in my head
I try to be you, instead
I get on the stage and paint my heart out
and yawn a song, no one knows anything about
I trek across the map not knowing
that where I go, you'll never be going
I have lunch with the birds, in the rain, in the spring
then I take launch again, to better things
inside myself I wither and die
as I try to be like you, instead of I

Weird

Goblins are rolling up and down these hills
Having fun and taking spills
Laughing at the sun and moon
Waiting for their supper soon

I see a man but he's half man, half monster
Am I scared?
Well, I'm not so sure
He's beautiful but terrifying all in one
He's horrifying like the night
But blinding like the sun

He leads them all up and down this hill
Then they all follow him down to the mill
He talks and they laugh and he seems so happy
I wonder if he's noticed me

They all sit down to dinner and offer him a piece off their plate
He looks full and satisfied although he still hasn't ate
They all leave the table and bow at his feet
And when he leaves the room, they too, retreat

I see them coming closer to me and I don't know what to do
I think I should run but I'm frozen in my shoes
Just as they come close enough I think about moving, maybe
But then the man that's half monster walks right through me

I look back and they're all gone and disappeared
If this isn't a dream, it sure is weird…

Words 2

Pounding
1
2
3

Tick
Tock
Misery

Insanity
Rolling

A
B
C

Moments

Voices
Screaming
Dead end
Choices

Breathless
A mess this is

Torture
Times up
So is temper

Temperature

Higher weather

Tick
Tock

1
2
3

Drowning in stale misery

Love

"I don't believe in soul mates, but if I did, I know you'd be mine." —CCV

A Painted Picture

The Earth shakes and the moon makes
A reflection on our skin
City lights and warm nights
Now our journey begins

My mind at ease, a cold breeze
You offer me your shirt
A long stare, the sweet smelling air
You wash away the hurt

Just as the tide does to the sand
Just with a touch of your hand
A familiar kiss, only this hasn't happened before
It's like de ja vu, but something more

I could never explain what my dreams are made of
Then there you go and tell me you're in love

A Wanted Wallflower

A wallflower amongst beauty queens
A shy girl in a party scene
I can't believe you plucked me out of the crowd
At the perfect hour
Me
The wallflower

It was a perfect night underneath Hawaiian stars
The ocean, the warmth, the beautiful cars
I saw you right across the street
This was a perfect night to meet
A few hours later in a hotel room
You called me to the balcony
To discuss my friend, I'd assume
To my surprise you leaned right in
I never would've known this could've been

A week of bliss
Ending in a romantic kiss
A long distant relationship
Longing for the way you bit your bottom lip
A year passed and finally I saw you

Amazing how much I never knew...

Cherry, Butter, and Your Eyes

Do you know that I see forever in your eyes?
As fire comes flying from the skies
And Mother Nature has no disguise
The cherry sunset
Doesn't let me forget
My former life and that one big regret
The sun looks like butter as it sinks down into the ground
And I cry when it's all the way down
Lighting strikes as the thunder rolls
All of this, she controls
No droplets fall from the sky
I sit, I watch, I wonder why
Yesterday I had you
The day was so long
Now I am here with the thunder and you are gone
Can you possibly hear the thunder too?
And can you hear what I whisper to you?
As I speak to you tonight
The wind takes my words and gives them flight
They fly with the leaves on their way to you
And I think about how much I never knew
But you opened your soul
And the words just like butterflies flew out
And you let me know what you're about
Cherry, butter, as my heart to you flies
Do you know I see forever in your eyes?

Eleventh of June

Do you remember the day you met me?
Was it love at first sight for you?
Because it was for me
When you first looked in my eyes
I was completely memorized

The stars were out and smiling was the moon
The night I met you was the eleventh of June

First, I saw you in paradise, just across the street
And I prayed to God that we'd get a chance to meet
My heart was somewhere better than cloud nine
You'd be forever mine

Seeing you again could never come too soon
That night I met you was the eleventh of June

Fell From the Sky

Fireworks going off just below the moon
I can't help think
That this is all happening a bit too soon
I try to do all the things I need to do
But I'm so damn wrapped up in you

Fell from the sky
And I won't lie
It hurt a little
Fell into you
Not sure what to do
And I think it feels good

Asking if you're ready isn't the only thing I fear
Wondering, not knowing
If this is the only reason you're here

Fell from the sky
And I won't lie
It hurt a little
Fell into you
Not sure what to do
But it feels good

Forbidden

When darkness comes and sun is sleeping
I touch myself instead of weeping
Knowing soon I'll be with you
I laugh and smile and this is what I do...

I want to touch you
But I know you're forbidden like the sun
I want to taste you
But I know you're like the apple in the Garden of Eden
That small forbidden one
I want to hold you
But I know you're like the forbidden stars
Hanging in the sky
I want to see you
But I know you're my only forbidden eye

Hello My Love

Hello my love
I've been waiting for you
I love you and you know it
I'm not afraid to show it

Good morning my love
I've been looking at you
I've been watching you too

Goodnight my love
My darling, my soul
I love you my darling,
More than you know

Key

He sits there in perfect serenity
One that is his own
He is normal, happy, and peaceful
But I've never felt so alone

He doesn't know the hell he puts me through
I'm not sure what I should do
I tell him but he just doesn't quite get it
Or he says he understands and then forgets it

We're just two different people in the same place
I fell in love from the moment I saw his face
I wear my heart on my sleeve but he hides his away
I hope and pray I get to see it someday

It's locked in a room, in a box, far from me
I hope that when I find it
I hold the right key…

Naked Truth

I saw you from across the street
I took the shoes right off my feet

In the night of Hawaiian air, I shook your hand
I took off my socks and threw them in the sand

I looked into your eyes and you looked right back
I felt a little chill in the air with out my pants

I felt your lips against mine on the balcony
And disappeared my blue tank top, the one that was small and flowery

I sat on your lap in the car while we replayed that song
Then gone was that little black thong

I told you I loved you and you didn't say it back
I felt naked and bare...I wish I wouldn't have said that

I didn't even sleep with you, and you didn't see me naked
I held onto that part of me that I held so sacred

What I'm telling you is each step I took with you
Revealed a little more of my Naked Truth

Quest for Paprika

He said, 'the only thing we'll miss is the thought of what could've been'
I guess that's why I love him
He's so wise in the funniest ways
He's good to me everyday

He said, 'I want to be on a quest for something,
how do you go on a quest?'
I smiled and kept driving, I tried not to cry, I gave it my best
But that's why I fell in love with him, in his most unusual phase
I fell in love with him in just six days

Because he told me to throw my couch in the pool
Because he thinks being 'estranged' and the word 'slumber' is cool

Because he says things like, 'let's go on a quest for paprika', and
'the only thing we'll miss is the thought of what could've been'
Because he's so oddly intelligent and annoying perfect
…That's why I love him

Rebirth

Both in the car
Your eyes as cold as the breeze beating on the door
Shadows creeping around
Talking to me, telling me to hurt you
As much as you hurt me
Your skin like cement
I know you are pushing away fate
My tears fall, as does the rain drizzle
I can hear it wind and rain on the roof
Never felt this pain
Not in any way
You hurt me
On purpose, you killed me
You don't want to
And I break down your wall
You are not strong enough to build it
As fast as I break it
A kiss from your steel lips
As you give in finally they turn to sugar
Victory is not mine, but ours
I know you now; the secrets out
We talk. We can
The lifestyle of yours can be over
And started with me
Your rebirth is in this car, this hotel room
The shadows disappear and you take the wall down yourself

Save Him

I wish I could save him from something
I wish he needed me
I wish I could be his strength, his shoulder to cry
on, and his bandage when he bleeds

I wonder if he'd be broken hearted if we couldn't be together
Or if he'd just assume we were both off better
I'm not sure if he depends on me, even a little, or even at all
I wonder if I walked away, I wonder if he'd fall

I wish I could protect him or take care of him
I wish he needed me
But the truth is I'm sure he'd do just fine, he wouldn't fall to his knees

I wish I knew how much he cared...or if he cared at all...
I wish I could save him from himself if he ever started to fall

The Day We Met

How could I forget the day we met?
When I touched you, I knew there was nothing I'd regret
Some people said we'd never be together
But I knew when I kissed you, that kiss meant forever

Seeing the seasons change without you was too much to take
But I knew giving up on you, put too much at stake
Feeling the cold was much worse without you
And feeling the warmth didn't feel as good as it used too

But I knew you'd come to me
And we'd be together endlessly
You might've thought meeting me would be something you'd forget
But I knew I loved you since the day we first met

They Say

They say that the miles matter
They say that the difference is too much
They say that our love is not stronger
Than the space between us

They say that the age between us matters
They say it will rip us in two
They say that our love is not growing
Because I am younger than you

They say that only time will tear us
They say the phone won't do
They say I cannot feel you
And that you will find someone new

But they are wrong
So far from being right
We will never give up
Never end the fight
I'll strive to be with you until you are mine
And you'll kill to be with me until the end of time

Those Two Named Romeo and Juliet

Star-crossed lovers
☆

Who was such a genius to write this!
To glorify death-not bliss
☆

An act of passion and love
Death by ones own hand
☆

A race to the death, literally
The seconds drop like sand
☆

Kin in an everlasting war
Star-crossed lovers settle the score
☆

What they did
It's what sins are made of
☆

Will they share afterlife in hell?
Or heaven?
☆

After all, it was a sin of love!

UGLY

I stare in this mirror with difficulty
Wondering how you love me?
I don't see what you see
Nothing pretty, nothing pleasing, no beauty

I see scars, although I have no torn tissue
Nothing's really wrong with me, that's the issue
I see burns, although its smooth across my skin
Good for me they say beauty is found with in

I reach out and touch the hideousness that I see
How is the monster really me?
I see nothing of purity, nothing of splendor
Nothing pretty or lovely, nothing tender

I look at my face, its jagged like pebbles
Like small little creatures on my face living like rebels
But when I feel it, its soft to the touch
How can you miss someone so disgusting...so much?

I see pain. I see suffering. I see agony.
How can someone like you...love someone like me?
You once told me just to look in the mirror and I'll see so much beauty...
Guess I just don't see what you see...

Maybe someday I'll see the beauty that you see in me
in this mirror
But I'm fairly certain...it won't be until you're here

Wake Up My Dear

Wake up my dear and tell me how you feel
And whisper something to me
Open your eyes and share something real
Try not to confuse me

Morning breaks through dirty window shades
Trying to hide but I know I can't
Running as the darkness fades

Wake up my dear and tell me what you think
Look in my eyes and try not to blink
Tell me something about your dreams
Or about your nightmares
No matter what your beliefs
I really do care

Wake up my dear and show me you're still alive
Wake up my dear; I'll try not to cry
Wake up my dear, lift your weary head
Open your eyes and get out of bed

What I Love About You

Smile when I make a stupid joke
Laugh when I cook and fill the house with smoke
Kiss me when my hair's a mess
Let me nap when I need the rest

All those little things you do
That's what I love about you

Say I look cute every time I cry
Tell me what shirts go good with my eyes
Touch my hand gently when I'm throwing a fit
Always stand, so I can sit

All those little things you do
That's what I love about you

Say I'm cute when I'm sad
Comfort me when I miss my dad
There are so many of those little things you do…
But you love me for me, and that's what I love most about you…

What I Love Most About You

You make me laugh at the dumbest things
I get the butterflies when the phone rings
You believe in Heaven and don't worry much about hell
You think it's pointless to throw pennies in the wishing well
You can eat a whole watermelon in just one night
You don't eat a lot, but drink everything in sight
You enjoy going car shopping and maybe do a few test runs
I'd have to say your favorite movie is definitely Young Guns
You have the sexiest smile I've ever seen
And you dressed as a pirate on Halloween

In your past you've done many things,
You've even been married before
But out of all those girls, I swear I love you more
You're loyal to your friends and love your family
And I just can't get over how well you treat me

Here are a last few things I love about you…

You love being a soldier and would fight to the death
You would give up everything for our son,
Even your very last breath
The fact that you take care of me better than anyone could
And you don't tell me you love me a lot but I'm not sure you should
Because every time you say it, I know it's really true
And every time I hear it, I fall more in love with you

28403101R00192

Made in the USA
Charleston, SC
12 April 2014